Catherine opens up the world of the Bible
as she brings alive the stories of six peo
shows how God didn't give up on them –
us. I especially appreciate how she reaches
tive and our minds with her teaching. Read, ponder, and savour this
delightful, trustworthy, and powerful book. You won't regret it.
Amy Boucher Pye, author of *7 Ways to Pray*

Catherine is an extraordinary woman. She is that women who is
acquainted with grief and loss, but her life is much richer than the
stories we know about her. Throughout the beautiful retelling of biblical
narrative in this book, she shows us that this is also the case for characters like Abigail, John Mark and Judah. Words like abuse, failure, guilt,
and ageing are turned around in our Creator's hand. Catherine and these
characters teach us about not giving up and trusting God for the rest of
our stories.
Debbie Duncan, author of *Gifted*

This book is as informative and inspiring as we have come to expect
from Catherine Campbell. Giving us a fresh insight into a selection of
Biblical characters, she draws us into a new understanding of the God
who spans history and his impact on our lives. This is a book for reading
and reflecting. You will want to go back and reread it anytime you find
yourself struggling and in need of encouragement. The practical questions for further study are ideal for individual or group study.
Jean Gibson, author of *Journey of Hope*

Catherine Campbell brings Bible characters to life, transporting us into
their narrative. Showing the individuals behind their stories, she gently
guides us to see who we are behind our own stories, and to meet God
there. Catherine points us to a God who never turns His back on us, even
when we try to run or hide. I laughed and I cried. I was also challenged,
reassured, and encouraged. I hope you will be, too.
Emily Owen, author of *Still Emily*

Dedicated to Billy and Silvia whose selfless involvement in the lives of others has encouraged many, including me.

GOD ISN'T FINISHED WITH YOU YET

Life lessons on not giving up

Catherine Campbell

INTER-VARSITY PRESS
36 Causton Street, London SW1P 4ST, England
Email: ivp@ivpbooks.com
Website: www.ivpbooks.com

© Catherine Campbell, 2022

Catherine Campbell has asserted her right under the Copyright, Designs and Patents Act 1988 to be identified as Author of this work.

All rights reserved. No part of this publication may be reproduced, stored in a retrieval system, or transmitted, in any form or by any means, electronic, mechanical, photocopying, recording or otherwise, without the prior permission of the publisher or the Copyright Licensing Agency.

Scripture quotations are taken from English Standard Version
Scripture quotations marked NKJV are taken from New King James Version
Scripture quotations marked NIV are taken from New International Version
Scripture quotations marked NLT are taken from New Living Translation

First published 2022

British Library Cataloguing-in-Publication Data
A catalogue record for this book is available from the British Library.

ISBN: 978–1–78974–422–4
eBook ISBN: 978–1–78974–423–1

Set in Minion Pro 9.75/12.25 pt
Typeset in Great Britain by Fakenham Prepress Solutions, Fakenham, Norfolk
Printed in Great Britain by Clays Ltd, Bungay, Suffolk

Produced on paper from sustainable forests

Inter-Varsity Press publishes Christian books that are true to the Bible and that communicate the gospel, develop discipleship and strengthen the church for its mission in the world.

IVP originated within the Inter-Varsity Fellowship, now the Universities and Colleges Christian Fellowship, a student movement connecting Christian Unions in universities and colleges throughout Great Britain, and a member movement of the International Fellowship of Evangelical Students. Website: www.uccf.org.uk. That historic association is maintained, and all senior IVP staff and committee members subscribe to the UCCF Basis of Faith.

Contents

A note from the author

I have thoroughly enjoyed retelling these stories from the Bible narrative for you. My aim has been to remain true to God's Word, while creating a picture that doesn't add to what is written but does provide context. I believe context enriches what we discover in the story, helping to bring the narrative to life. It lends a backdrop to what might otherwise be seen as an empty stage. However, the additional background is extensively researched from trusted sources. I don't just make it up! The social, political, and historical settings of each story are as accurate as I can make them – from the big details to the little ones. For instance, who could have imagined that the ancient Egyptians drank beer? I certainly didn't.

That is why I am extremely grateful for the many books, commentaries, and online resources that have assisted my writing. I am indebted to them for their knowledge, wisdom and inspiration, recognising that others have laboured, and *I* have entered into their labour (John 4:38).

Discouragement is only one of Satan's weapons, but an effective one. I have witnessed too many people crushed by life's burdens and give in to them, unable to see that God hasn't given up on them. That's why I wrote this book. I wanted you to read about Bible characters who survived, who discovered God's plan for them didn't end with their circumstances. I also wanted you to own this truth for yourself, because situations we view as detrimental can become a catalyst for spiritual change in our lives.

Including a 'Life lessons' section this time is different from some of my previous books (for example, *God Knows Your Name* and *When We Can't, God Can*). Instead of the reader drawing their own prayerful conclusions about what they should learn from the Bible adaptations – which will and should still happen – I decided to include key elements of helpful biblical teaching around the theme of each story. I hope you find it useful, alongside the opportunity for you to dig deeper with the addition of a personal, or group, study guide.

The adage of 'no man is an island' is certainly true when it comes to publishing a book. The author may feel alone for the greatest part of the process, but I can assure you there are plenty of others involved. My thanks go first and foremost to my patient husband, Philip. He is my sounding board, encourager, and prayer-partner, and he gets to be the first to read and comment (find the mistakes!) on my work. I couldn't have done this without him. And now, for the eighth time, my dear friend Liz Young has once more helped with her proofreading skills and advice – thanks Liz.

I am also very fortunate to have had the expertise of the team at Inter-Varsity Press to see this project through in such a professional manner, with special thanks going to my editor, Joshua Wells.

When I wrote my first book back in 2008 I had not planned to write another. However, I have been deeply humbled by the response to my books from readers, which is one of the reasons that my writing journey continues. Thank you for reading what I write, and more importantly, coming back for more. My goal is to write books that will challenge, encourage, and bring the reader into a closer relationship with God. I hope that *God Isn't Finished with You Yet* will do just that for you. Writing it certainly did it for me.

But it is to God alone that I bring my deepest thanks, grateful to Him for the enabling to complete this project during a time of great global, and personal, challenge.

God bless you… until next time.

Catherine can be contacted via:
Her website www.catherine-campbell.com
Facebook www.facebook.com/catherinecampbellauthor
Instagram @catherinecampbellauthor

Prologue

I was standing in line for the cash desk in a large department store. The queue was very long, of airport security line proportions, winding up and down between black bands positioned to keep order. While snaking along with the other shoppers I became aware of a woman looking at me. I smiled in response, but it soon became rather uncomfortable as she continued to stare.

At first I thought maybe I should know the woman. However, it soon became apparent that was not the case.

"I know who you are!" she shouted across two lines, her comments startling more than me. "You're that woman... that woman..."

I had no idea what she was going to say next, as she hesitated, trying to get her tongue around the words.

"... whose children died! Your children died, didn't they?"

I could sense bodies beside me stiffen, as heads including my own, dropped in embarrassment. Unfortunately she wasn't finished.

"I read your book. It was so sad. I cried..."

Never was I so glad to hear the words: "Next!" Nor indeed more thankful that the customer called forward was the lady who had just publicly shared my life with strangers.

Upset, but angry at the same time, I wanted to shout back. To tell this stranger that I was more than 'that woman' who had buried both of her daughters... to tell her that my life was marked by more than pain. In fact, she needed to know that I was more than the sum of my sad circumstances. But a condemning voice from deep inside told me to stay silent.

After all, you did write the book, taunted my accuser. *You put your life out there for all the world to see.* Instead of responding to the woman, now busy paying for her purchases, I made a hasty exit.

Sometime later, while attending a conference, I overheard a woman reply to a request for her to speak at a meeting about her recent battle with cancer.

"No, I'd rather not," she replied. "I don't want to be 'that woman'."

"Sorry, I don't understand," said the woman who had made the request.

"I don't want to be 'that woman' who allows her circumstances to define her. I am much more than a woman who has survived breast cancer."

I understood what she meant.

But, over the years, I had also experienced first-hand how God can take our suffering, even our sinfulness, and produce something positive from what we believed to be the ashes of our lives. Surveying life's ruins can make us think that God is finished with us. Our souls are saved, but that is all. We feel doomed – forever trapped by whatever ails us. We reckon that God can't possibly use spoiled or damaged goods. But quite the opposite is true for "God chose what is weak in the world to shame the strong" (1 Corinthians 1:27).

That's exactly what He did for the six people whose stories are retold in this book. Not one of them had it together as far as their lives were concerned. Weak doesn't even begin to describe them. Yet God used their situations to produce transformation. Abigail was trapped but God freed her. The Woman of Samaria was spoiled by sin but Christ forgave her. John Mark was a failure but God made him successful. Simeon and Anna were ageing but God made them useful. Judah was guilty but God changed him.

And Catherine Campbell was indeed 'that woman'… crippled by sadness and sorrow. But God did not leave me that way. Through it all He was present with me – caring, loving, and showing me that I was not defined by my circumstances, but that they would be used in transforming me into the image of His Son (2 Corinthians 3:18), with all that means. It's an ongoing process – one that will continue until the day I see my Saviour face to face. He's still working on me.

I am forever grateful that God does not leave us the way we are. While God Himself never changes (Hebrews 13:8), He is the One who brings about change in our lives. There is no one – and no circumstance, for that matter – that He cannot transform for His glory and for our good.

Please, don't give up. God isn't finished with you yet!

"'For I know the plans I have for you,' says the LORD.
'They are plans for good and not for disaster,
to give you a future and a hope.
In those days when you pray, I will listen.
If you look for me wholeheartedly, you will find me.'"
Jeremiah 29:11–13 (NLT)

I

TRAPPED
ABIGAIL

I

c. 1020 BC

The sun glinted off swinging swords as horsemen galloped across wool-carpeted fields in pursuit of the sheep stealers. Wild whooping and swirling dust scattered the panicked sheep, creating pandemonium in the normally quiet valley. The arrival of the horsemen triggered an eruption of fist-pumping delight from the haggard shepherds.

Watching four thousand sheep and goats was a nearly impossible task. With the sheep-shearing season almost on top of them, bringing the large flocks together so close to the shearing hall was unavoidable. But the wealthy owner of this mega flock accepted no excuses for lost sheep, whether by wolves of the four-legged kind, or two!

"Abba," shouted a young boy to the chief shepherd. "Did you see those men? Weren't they amazing, Abba?"

The child's words tumbled out in excitement, the bag hanging around his neck twisting as he hurried to unburden himself. The old man laughed at the child's predicament, reaching downwards to untangle the noose his grandson had managed to make of the lunch delivery bag.

"Who were they, Abba?" the boy continued, wide-eyed at what he has just witnessed. "Did you hire a guard so that the master wouldn't punish you, Abba?"

The child's words stung as the old man fingered the scar above his right eye. He didn't know what to say first: that it was his job to protect the flock for his master Nabal, or that, no, he hadn't hired guards to prevent the kind of beating he'd been dealt at last spring's shearing. Perhaps the Lord Jehovah had heard his prayer for the flock's safety after all.

"Yes, those men were brave, Ben," was the careful reply he offered to the inquisitive boy. "But they are simply neighbours with kind hearts and the ability to see off rascals who would dare to steal from a good man's flock."

Kneeling down he caught the boy in an embrace. "Where's the hug for your grandfather? It's been so long since I've seen you. What's your mother been feeding you?" he laughed, ruffling the child's dark curls affectionately. "I swear you'll soon be big enough to join me looking after the sheep."

"Really? Do you think so, Abba?" The boy's eyes danced at the thought. "Can I come with you after the sheep-shearing festival? Can I?" he pleaded.

With a cough and a rustling of the bag, the gentle, weather-beaten shepherd attempted a change of subject, and pulled the boy beside him onto the ground.

"So, what treats did you bring from that beautiful daughter of mine?"

Quickly the conversation changed to talk of family and fun as the two ate what seemed like a feast to the loyal shepherd. When the boy momentarily ran out of things to tell his Abba, the shepherd's mind returned to the few miles the flock had to cover before reaching the Judahite town of Carmel. Home – one he rarely saw, yet now so close he could almost smell his wife's bread baking.

But would he make it with the flock intact? Were those brave men still watching, or was a band of thieves waiting for them beyond the next hill? One thing was sure; he would keep young Ben close at hand, and personally deliver him into the arms of his mother. Sleep was hard to come by that night as the shepherd listened to the sounds of the wilderness. Gazing at the stars he took time to thank the God of David for sending protection, even if his master Nabal would spit at the sound of the name of Israel's anointed future king.

Abigail cringed at the sound of pots smashing on the ground. Two maids ran past crying as she headed in the direction of the commotion. It happened every year at this time. Nabal was always stressed as the sheep-shearing festival approached. His anger boiled over at the very thought that sheep might have been stolen, or lost, before they reached the shearing hall. Abigail marvelled that her husband had the ability to estimate the number in his flock with uncanny accuracy with a mere glance over the woolly multitude. Three thousand sheep and one thousand goats! But he expected every one of them to turn up for shearing. Pity the shepherd who lost any on the way home!

No, she thought, *she was wrong.* It wasn't only the sheep-shearing festival. Nabal could become angry at the sun in the sky if he set his mind to it. She could count on one hand the number of days since their wedding when Nabal *hadn't* been angry. In fact, it might not even need a whole hand.

"Can I help you, Nabal?" Abigail enquired, knowing only too well that there was little to assuage her husband's foul temper. She had learned to bow her head slightly and keep her words calm when Nabal's rage fired. And never to raise her voice in his company.

"You can beat those servants of yours with this!" he yelled, barely missing her with the stick he hurled in her direction. "Look at my robe! They can't even pour a man a drink in his own house without making a mess!"

"I will see to the stain, Master," she replied. "Everyone is a little nervous with the shearing almost on us. The staff are so busy making sure all is ready."

"I've told you before, woman, that you are too soft on those pathetic servants! Give them a beating or I will!"

"Master! Master!" Abigail was grateful for the boy's interruption. Distraction was needed before Nabal's fury became even more pointed. "They're here, Master!" the boy spluttered. "The sheep are on the horizon!"

"About time too!" Nabal growled. "There are a dozen shearers waiting."

Abigail kept her head low as her husband's large frame pushed past, requiring her to steady herself. She breathed deeply, glad that his mind was now on other things, yet dreading the drunkenness that would fill the days ahead. For now she needed to ensure the supply of food and drink never became an excuse to fuel the unmanageable behaviour of her churlish husband.

"Oh, Abba," she whispered as she sought out the master storekeeper. "Why did you choose this man for me? Was money really so important?" As quickly as those words fell from her tongue, Abigail's hands covered her heart: "I forgive you, Abba. I know you loved me."

It was late that night when Nabal returned home. Unusually his mood had moderated, and was almost pleasant. Apparently the flock had returned expanded by new life, and not unduly reduced by poaching. Nabal was not forthcoming as to how the loss was so small, but Abigail was pleased that their chief shepherd would avoid punishment this year – although she knew praise would be a step too far for her husband. Resting her head on sheepskin, she drifted off to sleep thankful to God that the day had ended better than most.

These days the sun rose too early for the ageing shepherd. The night watchmen had reported all was well although he wondered how that could be. Surely the noise of music and drunkenness from the continual partying that accompanied the annual shearing had unsettled the sheep... Still, the few weeks would pass soon enough. He would visit his wife, and then move on to search for fresh pasture as he had done for most of the days of his life since his youth. Soon one of the young men would take over. These days he felt the toll of a difficult life telling on his bones and he wasn't as able at dealing with the sheep stealers as he once had been.

"Good morning, Berel."

The shepherd startled, not having heard his master's approach as he walked the edge of the flock checking for wanderers.

"I didn't see you at the festival last night."

"Master," Berel replied, bowing low. "I visited my wife last evening. Our days together are few. I trust you are well?"

Their conversation was interrupted by the sound of horses coming alongside, attracting a few of the young shepherds to join Nabal and Berel in case there was trouble. Ten young men jumped to the ground, bowing respectfully before the rich merchant.

"Peace be to you, Master Nabal. Peace to your house, and peace to all you have."

Only Nabal looked sourly at the smiling visitors, the shepherds having recognised them from their frequent acts of heroism towards the master's flock, and their very lives too.

"We bring greetings from your servant David..."

Nabal's face contorted at the sound of that name, his hand moving over the gem-studded shank of the dagger tucked in his belt.

"Our master delights that your flock has safely reached shearing. He wishes you to know of the honour it was to help guard the flock and the lives of your shepherds so that neither were lost to reprobate men."

Berel stiffened, feeling his master's anger boil beside him. He knew that Nabal, a devoted follower of King Saul, would despise the thought that Saul's sworn enemy had anything to do with defending his sheep. The old shepherd dreaded his response but before he had time to diffuse the situation, some of his own young shepherds spoke up.

"Master, they speak the truth," they offered with enthusiasm. "Often they drove away the thieves, and undoubtedly saved our lives from those seeking to commit bloodshed. We were frequently grateful for their help."

Berel cringed. Nabal fumed.

"David asks," the visitors continued, "that you might now show us kindness by allowing us to have some food from your storehouse at this time of festival?"

The scar on Berel's forehead seemed to burn at the sight of his master morph into the monster the shepherd had encountered previously.

"W-h-a-t?" howled Nabal, his venomous words tripping over each other in their rush for air. "Who does David think he is that I should owe him anything? That... that... son of Jesse! That nobody!"

Berel's young shepherds stepped back in amazement at the verbal thrashing meted out by their master. Jaws dropped, eyes widened, but tongues were stopped by the wickedness of the one who had power not only to take their jobs from them, but their lives as well. Servants were expendable. Crestfallen, they listened on as Nabal's abuse continued.

"David! His name turns my stomach!" he continued. "David! The king's servant who wants his master's throne! He's no better than any other traitor!"

The horsemen, under instruction from their master to deliver a message and report back, offered no reply. Their silence was stronger than any of Nabal's vicious ranting.

"I will not waste the food I've prepared for my own on any of you! I'd rather give it to the pigs!"

The ten men remounted, leaving Nabal stamping on the ground like a small child in a temper tantrum.

Berel firmly stood his ground as Nabal's finger poked his ribs with such bruising force that it made his eyes water.

"Don't you ever let any scum of David's near my flock again!" Nabal shouted in the old shepherd's face. "I'd rather lose them all to thieves than be beholden to that enemy of our rightful king!"

The shepherds watched aghast as Nabal made his way back to the shearing hall, but Berel knew they hadn't heard the end of it, not by a long way.

As the cart bumped over well-grazed grass, Nabal's mind raced back to those recent days when Saul visited Carmel after his majestic defeat of the Amalekites. Hadn't he loaned some of his own men to help the king in the battle? Wasn't he first in line to welcome the conquering king to his hometown when he arrived to set up a monument to himself? *Surely great men shouldn't be denied a memorial to their triumphs,* he mused as the cart drew up alongside the shearing hall. *And if that interfering prophet Samuel hadn't spoiled Saul's party things would be different now! I'm glad that wretched prophet is dead!*

Nabal's head thumped in anger; too much wine and not enough sleep… or was it something else?

II

Abigail rose before her husband as she had done every day since they married. Her mother had taught her well. Since she was a little girl, she had learned the importance of being a good wife which included running a good home. She'd learned to bake the best of bread, as well as to mix spices such that even the cheapest piece of meat would taste good. She could weave with excellence, incorporating colours that brightened a room on the dullest of days. Memories of home frequently flooded her dreams and dropped out of nowhere, especially in the presence of flowers and beautiful things. Abigail's early life had been filled with beauty.

But what she loved best about her childhood was when her father would return home from business and sweep her off her feet, twirling her round until her head was spinning. Then they would giggle at her staggering until she was steady enough to run into his arms once more to experience his embrace. She had known only happiness and love… until the day she married Nabal.

Rarely had she heard her parents argue. Her mother loved and respected her father, but some unintentional eavesdropping enlightened Abigail to the marriage they were arranging for her.

"Nabal is a bully," her mother protested on that day when Abigail's life began to change. "I've heard it said at the market that he is unkind and greedy."

"Don't listen to all you hear from gossips, woman!"

Abigail's hand travelled swiftly to her mouth to stifle gasps that could not be held back as her father continued: "He is wealthy and can give her far beyond what we ever could."

"But…"

"No more, woman!" Abigail's father ended his wife's protesting with a few final words: "His bride price is handsome and ready for exchange, and I have worked hard to present a dowry larger than most."

Before running off into the shadows, Abigail heard her mother sob and the gentle man she knew and loved speak in kinder tones, "Don't worry, my love. Abigail will be good for Nabal. She knows how to show love… perhaps that's all he needs." But the silence between them spoke louder than the words exchanged. "I believe this is for the best. I would never do anything to harm our child. She is my joy."

She is my joy.

Those were the words that had sustained Abigail since the wedding feast. The words that kept her heart soft on the days when she wanted to run away. When her coarse-mannered husband called her names she tried to imagine it as coming from the man whom she knew truly loved her. Oh how she wished she could see her father right now. Ask his counsel. Feel the warmth of his heart towards her. Instead, she vowed to make him proud. Be the woman and the wife he would want her to be.

So every day *her father's joy* would rise and be the best she could be, listening in her head to her mother's voice offering the wisdom she needed to run the house of the wealthiest man in Carmel. Who knows? Maybe Nabal could be taught to love as her father had said. Up until now, she was barely more to him than any of the servants he hired or owned. The concept of relationship was lost on the man whose only thought was wealth and power. At times, Abagail even wished she wasn't beautiful – for Nabal enjoyed speaking of her beauty with other men in an unseemly fashion. Her husband loved to make her blush and didn't care if he made her unhappy.

On the worst of days, Abigail felt trapped.

There was no way of escape from the miserable life she had with this crass, unkind, specimen of humanity. But Nabal was her husband, meaning that both law and duty bound her to him. And so, in spite of this, Abigail chose to do her best for her husband and their household. God's laws weren't harsh requirements. They were a reminder of all the Lord Jehovah did for a frequently ungrateful people during the Exodus wanderings, and since their arrival in the Promised Land. Nabal may not have been deserving of her loyalty and service, but the merciful God she'd heard about at her mother's knee certainly was.

Her mother had impressed on her that privilege came with responsibility: something that Abigail was not prepared to shirk. She determined that her house would be the best run in the district, and that her household would be treated with respect and kindness. So, each morning, she washed her face and greeted her staff with a smile – something they warmed to in what had previously been a house of fear.

As the servants observed her interactions with their master, they discovered they could trust her, for wisdom and grace seemed to follow their brave mistress' every step. Such attributes led to trust and to the resolution of many of her husband's misdemeanours before they got out of hand. Like the day Nabal's servant rushed Abigail out of the kitchen at the start of the shearing festival.

III

The smell of roasting lamb delighted Abigail almost as much as the appetites of sheep shearers surprised her. The storekeeper had been working closely with his mistress for months in preparation for the annual feast that saw a doubling of the staff they needed to feed – to say nothing of the constant flow of guests Nabal invited to view the spectacle. The store of raisins, figs, flour, roasted grain, olives, oil, spices, and salted meats was piled high, but even so, Abigail wondered if they'd have enough for what she hoped would be no longer than a week.

Long before dawn the women busied themselves baking a mountain of bread. Abigail's bigger concern was over the size of Nabal's wine store – such was its size that a guard had to be posted on it day and night. Feeding this multitude was, in many ways, a pleasure, but her husband was too fond of the taste of wine at any time. The flow of it increased substantially at times of celebration, rendering him – and many others – unpredictable to say the least.

The shearers worked long and hard with a constant audience of little boys who were mesmerised at the men's ability to still these jittery animals while removing their thick woollen coats in one piece. The four black dots marked in the shape of a diamond on the sheep's necks denoted Nabal's ownership – and, therefore, quality – making the fleeces more expensive for buyers. Many a dream was formed in young hearts at the sight of such skill.

Passing the pile of fleeces already shorn caused Abigail to rub her neck. Sometimes it felt as if those dots had also been branded onto her.

She was, after all, just another of Nabal's acquisitions. With a sigh, she made her way to the expanded row of cooking fires to help with the bread-making. The supply of loaves never seemed enough with all those mouths they had to feed!

Her appearance met with respectful bowing and smiles. Not only could she work as hard as the best of the bread-makers, but her presence ensured that the men left the women alone. And Abigail loved to be with the women. And the little ones playing close by caused her mood to lift. Time passed quickly as the mountain of bread rose amid the friendly chatter of busy women.

The pleasant bustle was suddenly interrupted by the arrival of one of Nabal's young servants. Flustered and anxious, he bowed low before his mistress, large drops of sweat dripping off his nose with the downward tilt of his head.

"Mistress," he said, unable to hide his distress. "I need to speak with you urgently… and privately."

The chattering stopped, and was replaced by a cloud of concern as Abigail rose to her feet. Zach was wise beyond his years and the mistress of the house respected the young man's work and wisdom. He was one of her husband's personal servants – a man Nabal trusted in the business as well as the household. Abigail reckoned that her husband was training Zach for more important duties, as he had recently been called on to accompany Nabal on his business trips. There was little about his master that the young Zach didn't know. But as they stepped towards the storehouse, Abigail had no idea what was causing his agitation.

She'd never seen Zach in such a state. His hands shook like palm trees in a windstorm. His tongue stuck in his mouth, behind lips that grew paler by the second: his clothes soaking with sweat. He could barely stand for the weakness that swept over him. Abigail grabbed his arm, pushing him down atop an overturned pot.

"Zach, breathe," she said as calmly as she could, holding his hands in hers to stop the violent tremor.

"We are doomed, Mistress," he croaked. "Doomed."

Perplexed, Abigail ran to a water pot standing tall in the corner, spilling as much on the floor as she'd managed to retrieve in her ladle.

"Drink this, Zach. Settle yourself and tell me what's happened."

The water loosened his dry tongue, but still he stumbled over his words.

"Some of David's men visited the master when we were checking the unshorn sheep just now."

David. The Lord's anointed future king. His very name made Abigail's heart jump with pride. She hadn't been married to Nabal when King Saul came to Carmel after the battle with the Amalekites, but she had heard of how Saul had been rejected by the Lord because of his disobedience. And now with the prophet Samuel dead the people desperately needed a king they could trust to do what was right in the eyes of the Lord.

David. Here… in Carmel?

"His men have been protecting our sheep," Zach continued. "Not one of them was lost as the flock skirted the wilderness on their way back to Carmel."

So that's how the flock was not depleted, Abigail mused as the lad continued. Nabal kept that quiet.

"They chased the thieves! Killed the wolves! They became like a wall that no one could scale, keeping the flock safe." Zach was animated now, stopping only briefly to gulp down the remaining water. "And they demanded no payment."

"But that's wonderful, Zach," Abigail interrupted. "Why is this *bad* news? How could we be doomed?"

"Because the m-master," Zach stammered, "fool that he is, refused their mannerly request for food now that the festival is upon us!"

Zach gasped at his own disrespectful words, his hand shooting over his mouth as he waited for his mistress' rebuke. Instead, she shook her head urging him to continue. If there was one thing she did know, it was that Nabal was well named, "Fool"!

"And that wasn't all! The master fumed, denouncing David's heritage and speaking ill of David's family." There was no stopping Zach now, seeing his mistress pale at the horror of his account. "He went so far as to call David a disreputable fellow as if he was just like any other rebel seeking to take power from his rightful master!"

He said what? Abigail shook her head in disbelief. Just when she thought her husband could do nothing more to shock her, the next faux pas would burst on the scene.

"Mistress!"

Zach's urging yanked her from her thoughts.

"Did David's men attack your master for his folly?" A sudden picture of Nabal dead at the feet of those he had offended raced across her mind.

"No, Mistress. They acted respectfully at all times."

"Then why are we doomed, Zach? I don't understand."

"They were obviously sent to deliver a request which they hoped would result in some payment," the servant offered. "I doubt a simple refusal would have caused the difficulties we are now in. The Master insulted the future King of Israel, Mistress! It is said David has a small army encamped with him... men who have already put their own lives on hold for him."

Abigail began to get the picture, and it wasn't pleasant.

"David will attack, Mistress! I have no doubt he will feel compelled to avenge his good name!" Zach filled his lungs one last time knowing his life depended on how his final words came out. "Mistress, there is no talking to that scoundrel Nabal! You've got to do something or we are all doomed... there won't be one of us left alive tomorrow!"

The sound of Abigail's thumping heart seemed to echo off the storehouse walls. Zach was right. There would be no talking to Nabal. Something had to be done. But was she strong enough to do what was needed?

I am as trapped as the others who work in this household. He is my husband. I am commanded to respect and obey him. If I go against him, Nabal might kill me! A battle raged in Abigail's mind, her mother's words as loud and clear as if she were standing right beside her: Remember, my daughter, you must never do anything to dishonour your husband.

"Mistress!" Zach's voice interrupted the panic and confusion. "Mistress, we must do something!"

Another voice echoed in the inner recesses of both mind and heart. It belonged to her beloved Abba: *Abigail,* his strong yet gentle voice spoke through the chaos. *Abigail, you must "Love the Lord your God with all your heart".* A tear escaped down her flushed cheek as the words from the Law filled her to the brim. Abba recited those precious words daily as she had grown up – words she hadn't heard since she'd left his home. Yes, she must obey her husband, but her priority must be to put God first.

"Thank you, Abba," she whispered, pushing away the tears, and startling Zach into searching the room for the one she was talking to.

And neither of them had heard someone else enter the storehouse. On discovery, Mishael, the master storekeeper raised his hand to assure them they were not in danger.

"I heard everything Zach said." Coming closer and bowing low to his mistress, he continued, an urgency sounding in his lowered voice, "We will help you, Mistress. Do you have a plan?"

Oh how Abigail loved this older man whose wisdom and decorum matched her father's so closely! Drawing both of them into a close circle, she felt strength rise – not just from them, but also from the One whose help they sought before uttering another word to each other. Abigail wanted bloodshed to be averted, but she longed for God's glory above all else. Nabal may be a son of Belial, but she was a daughter of Jehovah.

The threesome set to work, drawing together Abigail's plan to avert disaster. She would go to David herself, and grovel if she had to. Her servant-family would not die today if she had anything to do with it. And the brave young woman dared not stop to think of the consequences of her actions. She was on God's business.

Zach headed off to acquire the aid of some trusted friends, hoping that the donkeys they planned to use in the mistress' plan would behave and stay quiet. Abigail was glad of the storekeeper's strength as they gathered together the gift she would offer to David. Managing to secrete such an amount away without Nabal, or others, seeing it would require the help of Heaven, she thought, as the stack of food grew.

Suddenly, the familiar roar of her husband stopped the twosome in their tracks. Abigail ran for cover behind a tower of grain sacks.

"Mishael! Where are you, you dog!"

Abigail's heart almost stopped for fear. *If he finds us here. Now. We are doomed, just as Zach said.*

"M-mish…"

"I'm here, Master."

Abigail stifled a gasp as she heard her brave storekeeper close the door of the store behind him, blocking Nabal's entrance.

"I was checking that everything was ready for tonight's banquet."

"Come when I call you!" Nabal screeched, pressing his bulbous nose into Mishael's face.

"I beg your pardon, Master."

Listening from her hiding place Abigail prayed that Nabal wouldn't strike her dear servant, a regular occurrence in Nabal's day.

"We need more wine! Now!"

"Yes, Master, right away."

Abigail sighed as she pictured the storekeeper's low bow, waiting for his master to release him to the task.

Nabal's need for wine at this time of the morning was undoubtedly fuelled by the excessive adrenaline produced by his encounter with David's men. Arrogance obliterated any sense of wrongdoing in Nabal. Saul owed him, and as he swaggered away from yelling at the storekeeper, he looked forward to his loyalty being rewarded by Israel's king. Pointless pride pushed his head high into air, dropping it only to spit in the dust at the echo of David's name in his mind.

When she was sure Nabal had gone, Abigail returned to gathering the supplies. Work was slower now that she was left to do it on her own, and she knew it was impossible for her to lift the sacks of grain. Yet she hoped the storekeeper would not return. She needed him to ensure her husband was occupied while she finished her mission.

Sacks filled with bread as word was whispered along the row of women to bake faster and hide the reducing piles by their fires. *Two hundred loaves should be enough. Figs. The same number of cakes perhaps?* Abigail's counting was suddenly interrupted by men bursting through the door! Legs wobbling, her head spun like a child's top on hard ground. *She'd been found out!*

"Mistress, it's all right. You're safe." Zach's voice, and strong arms, stopped her from sliding to the floor. "These men are going to help us. They are sworn to secrecy. The master will never know."

Oh he'll know all right. But she would be the one to tell him. Just not now…

As she gathered herself together, Abigail remembered the Lord's words to Joshua as he set out on a much more dangerous journey than she was about to make. "Be strong and of good courage," He had told the brave general. "Do not be afraid, nor be dismayed, for the Lord your God is with you wherever you go" (Joshua 1:9 NKJV). And the words washed over her soul like rain on a hot day. What she was about to do was not merely to save her household. God's glory was at stake. That was something worth risking her life for.

Soon the donkeys were loaded, and never had she seen such quiet beasts! Bread. Figs. Raisins. Roasted grain. And five dressed sheep ready for a feast. Could it possibly be enough to placate David? Abigail hoped so. Just as the last sack was placed on the beasts of burden the storekeeper arrived, breathless and sweating, carrying two skins of wine – their finest, no doubt.

"Mishael! Were you seen?"

"No Mistress," he replied hurriedly, attaching the wineskins to the lead donkey. "The master is too engrossed in the exaggerated tale-telling of loyalty to King Saul to notice I'd gone, but I must return before I am missed."

The storekeeper bowed low as Abigail wrapped a covering around her jewel-combed hair.

"Godspeed, Mistress," Mishael said, "and may He give you success."

Abigail smiled, thankful in the knowledge that her faithful servant would keep Nabal so busy with feasting that he would not miss her. Hopefully.

IV

Abigail had instructed Zach and the other men to go on a short distance ahead of her. She didn't want to meet David surrounded by a band of men. She intended their encounter to be as non-threatening as possible… and respectful. The young woman couldn't undo her husband's insolent comments but she hoped her deference to David might dampen the fire in his heart for revenge.

Zach had a general idea of where David and his men had camped. In spite of the fact that they often moved from one natural stronghold to another, he told his mistress where they would be sure to meet David and his four hundred men.

Abigail and her band of helpers managed to leave Carmel without drawing much attention to themselves. Only once had she heard her husband's guffaw fill the air as they took the winding back road away from their homestead and towards the wilderness. The sound was enough to send shivers down her spine yet a sense of peace quickly pushed the fear away. Keeping her eyes on the donkeys ahead, she followed the edge of the flock, the afternoon sun casting shadows on the rocky hills to her left.

Zach fell back to check that his mistress was okay. He brought her bread, convinced that she couldn't have eaten since rising earlier on this most difficult of days. It was hard to imagine his mistress riding a donkey like a farmer's wife, yet here she was, desert dust clinging to her beautiful face, putting herself in danger for the likes of him. *She deserves better,* the young man thought as he offered her the bread… *definitely better than Nabal.*

"Thank you, Zach," his mistress said, but with a kind determination told him, "I won't let anything pass my lips this day until our task is complete."

Bowing his head, Zach returned to the front of the little caravan, his heart enlarged further with pride for his mistress.

Repeatedly, Abigail rehearsed in her head what she was going to say to David. Would they even stop when they saw her beleaguered little gang? Would David listen to a woman? Would he take any notice of the wife of a Saul-follower... the wife of the man who had insulted him and his family? The heat began to cause her head to spin. The nearby mountains promised the shade she needed as she encouraged her little donkey to move a little faster.

No sooner had they entered the ravine Zach had spoken of than she saw those ahead of her move to either side, opening a path for her to pass through. That's when she saw him. Young. Handsome. Bronzed by the sun. The strong look of authority she had always imagined he would have. Leading his men... from the front.

David. The Lord's anointed. The future king of Israel.

So much passed through her mind in those brief moments, his aura such that Abigail had no hesitation in sliding from her donkey and falling at his feet. Before David could speak, words tumbled out of her mouth like water over a cliff.

"My lord, I know my husband Nabal is a wicked man. His very name describes his character – he is foolish beyond belief. If you want to blame anyone, my lord, then blame me. I didn't know of your request until too late or I would gladly have rewarded your men for the kindness they showed to our shepherds."

Four hundred men stopped dead at the sight of this brave woman. Their silence allowed her words to echo through the mountain pass. Zach shook at the madness of what he was witnessing. David's men could kill them all in a moment. Yet, the sight of her in the dust, repenting of something she didn't do, quelled the anger of Nabal's enemies like kicking dust over a burning fire.

No one dared interrupt. Not even David.

"As surely as the Lord lives."

A woman who speaks of the Lord. She had David's ear.

"As surely as the Lord lives, who has protected you from shedding blood in personal vengeance, He will deal with your enemies, my lord. Don't let the blood of this scoundrel Nabal blemish your record."

Stopping for breath, Abigail spread her arms towards the heavily laden donkeys: "See, my lord, I have brought you a gift, to be enjoyed by all these young men who follow you."

The men behind David began to nod, while David's hand had, by this time, dropped from his dagger. But Abigail wasn't finished.

Bowing her head to the ground once more, she pleaded with Israel's future king to forgive her and offered a blessing on his head.

"You are safe in the treasure pouch of the Lord our God," Abigail reminded him. "Those who search for you can do you no harm, for the Lord will make your dynasty great as He has promised. He will destroy your enemies as swiftly as a stone flies from a sling. Allow God to avenge. Have no regrets, my lord, when you come to your throne."

Abigail felt her heart race as she completed her plea for mercy: "And when the Lord has done these great things for you, perhaps you will remember your servant."

Had she done enough?

Zach sensed the atmosphere had changed in that narrow place between the mountains. Yet no one moved. *Should he direct the donkeys forward?* He glanced either side for some advice but his fellow servants were struck dumb. His mistress remained on her knees before the Lord's anointed. Nothing was happening. He didn't know how much more his heart could take. The seconds seemed like hours before the tense silence was broken.

"The God of Israel has surely sent you to me today. Praise to His name!"

David's voice was now the one filling the rocky amphitheatre, causing a wave of relief to relax shoulders and minds on both sides.

She'd done it! There will be no bloodshed today! Pride for his mistress filled the young servant as the man he would one day gladly bow to as king continued to speak.

"Your wisdom has saved the life of your foolish husband, and has also saved me from taking vengeance out of God's hands and into my own."

Abigail almost collapsed with relief, her face so close to the ground that she felt she was inhaling the dust. But it was worth it to hear those words.

"God is my judge," David said, humility adding inches to his stature, "for if you had not rushed to meet me here not one of Nabal's men would have survived until morning. Because of you, blood has been spared, as well as my integrity."

Nodding in the direction of the gifts they had brought, David thanked Abigail for her kindness. Within minutes, Abigail and her servants were alone once more in the rocky ravine. While her young men backslapped each other in celebration, Abigail wept.

What would become of her now?

V

Disaster had been averted.

The stress of the day had reduced Abigail to little more than a rag doll. She could barely hold herself upright on the donkey. Her heart was bursting as it vacillated between the thrill of saving so many lives and the fear of facing her husband with what she had done. Yet regret was not one of the emotions vying for her attention. She knew she had done the right thing. And the God of Israel had made it all possible. Jehovah's honour and David's integrity had both been maintained. She had, however, pronounced her husband a scoundrel in public; worse still, she had done so to someone he would call an enemy. She had made him look foolish.

He did that all by himself, my dear one. Leave him to Me.

The gentleness of the voice within calmed her somewhat, renewing her strength as the lights of home pierced the darkness ahead. There would be consequences to face for sure. She just hoped her servants would not be punished, so she practised a different speech on the journey home.

Nabal had not even missed Abigail. He'd spent the afternoon recounting how he'd put David in his place. No doubt the story had been embellished with each telling. Whatever their politics, few of Nabal's guests would rebuke him for his folly. His friendship, if it could be called such, was essential for them to stay in business in Carmel. If Nabal blacklisted you, you might as well put a dagger to your own throat for you would surely starve. His kind of power couldn't be taken lightly. And anyway, his parties were legendary.

For once, Abigail was glad that Nabal's party went on long into the night, and even that Mishael hadn't watered the wine. She slipped past her husband and his drunken buddies, shook off the desert dust and lay down her weary head. What she had to tell him needed him to be sober. It could keep until morning.

And God gave His beloved sleep.

The sun was up long before Nabal was.

The sheep were still bleating. The children still playing. Life was continuing in spite of Abigail's terror for what lay ahead. And the women's smiles, though sincere, hid behind them a concern for their mistress as she sat for a short time to bake her husband's favourite bread, filled with rosemary and goat's cheese. She would give him a good breakfast... and then tell him. Scanning the row of bakers, it was obvious that Zach hadn't been able to keep the happenings of the previous day to himself. Abigail needed to tell Nabal before someone trying to garner her husband's favour reached him first.

She oversaw the master's breakfast tray. It was filled with hot bread, cheese, figs, and those plump juicy raisins that he loved. All perfectly placed on a silver platter, decorated with wildflowers and herbs. It looked and smelled delicious. Abigail knew Nabal had to eat well to counter the effects of the previous night's alcohol. She needed him to have a clear head before she made her confession.

Nabal's house servant was dispatched with the food and Abigail went off to a quiet place to compose herself. She had fleeting thoughts of keeping her meeting with David secret. Surely, Nabal didn't need to know. He could think he'd got away with his folly, and no one would get hurt. But her Abba's words "honesty makes the finest clothing" wouldn't leave her. If she didn't own up then, she would bring shame to her father – and that would break her heart. Anyway, Nabal had enough people of like mind around him to discover the truth for himself. That would be much worse.

If I was brave enough to face David, then I can surely face Nabal!

Abigail straightened her robe, and ran her fingers over her braided hair. She was ready.

Be strong, dear one, whispered the Voice from deep within her soul. *I will deal with Nabal.* And His words added pace to her steps and peace to her trembling heart.

"Good morning, my lord," her voice trembled slightly from the doorway. "May I enter and speak with my husband?"

Nabal grunted, gesturing her to enter. He'd managed to prop himself up on a multitude of silk pillows, his mouth full of the sumptuous breakfast she had prepared. Abigail waited to have her husband's attention, convinced he could hear the now frantic beating of her heart.

Help me, Lord.

"What do you want, woman? Can't you see I'm busy?"

A spray of raisins left Nabal's mouth along with his words, the dried fruit by far the sweeter of the two.

Abigail had learned not to be startled either by Nabal's lack of table manners or by his brusque responses. She readied herself, however, for the shock he would receive with her reply.

"Where were you last night, Abigail?" His eyes glanced in her direction for the briefest of seconds. "Can't a man expect his wife to be at his side for the biggest celebration of the year?"

It was time for Nabal to hear the truth.

"I was on my lord's business," she replied, her words strong and clear as she straightened in front of the rascal.

"My business?" Nabal hollered. "I do not send a woman to do my business!"

She had his attention now, the tray of food flying across the floor as he continued: "What business could you possibly be doing for me?"

Now was not the time to weaken.

"I was saving your life, my lord. Your business. Your property. Your servants. I went to see David, the Lord's anointed."

"You did w-h-a-t?"

Now she'd started Abigail had no intention of being interrupted. She had learned the art of assertion with respect, something missing from her husband's interactions with others.

"I had heard of my lord's unfortunate response to David's request for food in respect of guarding your flock. It needed to be put right before revenge was taken. Before blood was shed."

Nabal opened his mouth – but, for the first time ever, he was dumbfounded. Couldn't speak... as if a hand covered his lips. Abigail took the advantage and related the previous day's events with staccato precision.

"We cannot oppose the Lord's anointed, Nabal. And David has an army of four hundred men willing to do anything at his command, especially to maintain his good name."

She had his attention, Nabal's arrogance retreating behind startled eyes.

"His request was not unreasonable but your response was unforgiveable in his eyes. I took him gifts of food and some wine... and just in time, my lord."

Abigail's apparent respect for her husband, while at the same time exposing his failures was like a dagger to the core of Nabal's soul. But it was the size of David's army that literally grabbed the merchant's heart. Nabal could barely breathe as his wife continued.

Four hundred men!

"We met his army in the ravine just beyond the farm. They were angry. Ready for revenge. Baying for your blood! And for the blood of every innocent man in your household!"

Abigail felt her anger rise at the thought of what might have been. She breathed a silent prayer that she might finish with the same grace that God, and David, had shown to her. But something was happening. She had never seen her husband so pale. So quiet. She needed to finish but she wouldn't and couldn't smooth over the magnitude of what she'd put herself through for him, her servant-family, and ultimately God's glory.

"I grovelled in the dust at David's feet, Nabal. Begged his forgiveness – was prepared to take the blame for you. But do you know what prevented our end, Nabal?"

Sweat ran in rivulets down Nabal's face. His cheeks the colour of sun-bleached stone. Pride had been put in its place. Egotism buried in the food stains of his cloak.

"David bowed to my pleas to follow God's law, not to allow vengeance to smear his record with the God who will one day place him on Israel's throne. My lord, he is without doubt a man after God's own heart. Something you know nothing about."

There. It was said. Finished. Abigail's heart was cleansed from any deception she might have been accused of. God had given her the strength, and dignity, to do what was right. She bowed low before her husband, waiting for his anger to explode on her.

Silence.

She stood bowed before the man who had the power to take her life. Yet the only voice she heard was audible to her alone.

Well done, My child.

Still there was only silence.

"Mistress, Mistress."

Abigail opened her eyes to the pleading of Nabal's personal attendant.

"Mistress, something is wrong!"

His anxiety filled the space between Abigail and the master's bed.

"The master... something is wrong!"

Gasping, Abigail ran to her husband's side. At first she thought he was dead, but holding her cheek close to his mouth she could feel her husband's shallow breathing. His arms dropped like stones to his sides as she felt his cold hands. Saliva ran down his chin like a baby. His face contorted on one side. His mouth drooping low.

Have I killed him? Did my words do this, Lord?

Abigail's hands covered her face as she tried to think what to do, her confused mind repeating the words she had spoken to David only the day before. God would destroy his enemies as swiftly as a stone flies from a sling.

Is this what God's judgment looks like?

Nabal's servant was still jumping around pleading with her to do something. But Abigail didn't know what to do. Sending him for water was all she could think of – and to urge him to bring help to make their master more comfortable.

The servants treated Nabal with dignity and respect, even those who had felt the wrath of his anger on occasion. Abigail was proud of them as she watched their gentle care of him for ten long days. Those with a mastery of healing herbs made various concoctions and rubs attempting to rouse their master from his deep sleep, but all to no avail.

The compound worked on with the silence of angels' wings as Abigail sat in God's waiting room with her husband. Even the sound of children's laughter seemed respectfully muted. The shearers finished without fanfare. The flocks moved on to fresh grazing. All was quiet when God took Nabal's final breath from his body. The fool would never belittle another soul again. Never presume himself master of his own destiny. Yet Abigail was sad. Sad for a life that could have been so much more.

And now she was a widow. Even in death Nabal had her trapped – for that was all she would ever be: Nabal's widow. Wrapped in black for the rest of her days.

"Are you finished with me too, Lord?" she would whisper on her dark days. "Is there no more for me to do?"

"Mistress, Mistress!"

Zach ran across the compound searching for Abigail. She rushed towards the sound of his voice concerned at the young man's tone.

"Mistress, riders on the horizon! Galloping in this direction!"

As he stopped to catch his breath, Abigail made her way to the gate to catch a glimpse of the travellers. Things had been so quiet since her husband was laid in the tomb. Sure enough, horsemen were not far from her home. Mishael pulled her away from the gate and back towards the house.

"Mistress, we do not know what their intentions are. You need to stay safe until we see what they want."

But it was too late. The riders entered the compound before her retreat, causing Mishael and Zach to position themselves between the mistress and the horsemen.

The riders dismounted and dropped respectfully to their knees, heads bowed before the woman in black. Abigail moved her self-appointed guards aside and welcomed them to her home.

"Bring wine for our guests, Mishael," Abigail commanded. "And food. Where are your manners?"

The leader of the horsemen rose to his feet.

"We bring greetings from our master, David."

David!

She hadn't heard of David since the encounter in the ravine.

"I trust your master is well," she replied, hoping they didn't hear the nervousness in her voice. "How can we be of assistance to your master?"

"My master has no request but one, Mistress."

Abigail gestured the young men to the shade of a tree where they sat together under its branches. Once seated, Mishael had servants plying them with wine, figs, and fruits, eastern hospitality dictating the protocol before business could be discussed. The minutes felt like hours to Nabal's widow, whose hands trembled around the cup Mishael had placed into her hands.

The young men ate as if they had never seen food, their hunger an indication to Abigail of what life on the run must look like. She let them fill their bellies until she could wait no longer.

"You have a message from your master for me?" she enquired, the nervousness in her voice getting their attention.

The leader of their band jumped to his feet as if remembering they had come for something other than food.

"Mistress," he said, clearing his throat. "My master David has but one request to make of you today…"

You've said that already, Abigail thought, longing that he would get around to telling her what his master wanted. *Perhaps food?*

"To ask you," he said, stopping to clear his throat, "to become his wife."

A sudden gasp travelled around the compound with the speed that lightning strikes the earth, while Abigail struggled to regain both composure and decorum.

Wife. To the future king of Israel. Me?

The ground seemed to move beneath her as she rose to her feet. David's emissary stood silently, head slightly bowed, awaiting her reply, while her faithful staff looked on wide-eyed and dumbstruck.

"It would be my honour," she replied with the gentle grace she had shown all of her short life. "Even to wash the feet of David's servants would be my delight."

Abigail didn't see Mishael hurry off or Zach's face change from delight to sorrow. She only saw a future ahead for her. A future she recognised would not be easy, at least not until David was crowned king, but one which involved her as wife to a man who loved God. A man she could respect. A man she could love.

There was little time for goodbyes. David's men had been instructed to bring Abigail back with them. As they enjoyed yet more food Abigail quickly gathered what could be carried by a donkey, thankful that five of her young servants were willing to come along as her personal attendants. Tears flowed as she quickly took her leave. The people gathered at the gate had shown her love and acceptance while she lived with a man who had shown her neither. But soon Nabal's family would arrive to assume responsibility for the household and business. She prayed they would be nothing like the previous master.

Her eyes said all that was needed to Zach and Mishael. She couldn't have done what she had without their faithful and sacrificial service.

"May the God of Israel bless your lives and households with His peace," was all she could manage as she left Nabal's home for the final time.

The afternoon sun brightened more than just the sky as the brave Abigail left her place of entrapment to journey into the next adventure that the Lord Jehovah had planned for His servant.

And Abigail was at peace.

Adapted from the story told in 1 Samuel 25:1–42.

Trapped: Life lessons

The struggle

Three thousand years ago, life was very different to what it is today. Marriages were arranged, often from childhood. Betrothal was a legal arrangement as compared with the rather informal promise of engagement today. The couple may have met before the wedding, especially if they grew up in the same village. But more often than not, they remained strangers until the day when the young woman left her father's home to become a bride. From that day on, she lived with her husband's family, under her husband's authority. There was no running back home if you weren't happy with your father's choice of a groom.

However, Hebrew men and women had strict guidelines as to how they were to fulfil their married roles. Men generally attended to the business, and provided for their family, while the women looked after their household and brought up the children. Interestingly, even though it was a patriarchal society, the Law of Moses stated that children were to, "Honour your father **and** your mother" (Exodus 20:12 emphasis mine) indicating a respect for women that neighbouring societies did not have. Love often followed commitment, but was not considered a prerequisite for marriage.

Abigail's husband, Nabal, was a Hebrew but obviously not a follower of Jehovah, in spite of being from the godly and noble family of Caleb. In fact, he is literally described as "a son of Belial" (1 Samuel 25:17 KJV) – a worshipper of the god Bel, later a term used for Satan. His harsh, rude, ill-tempered, and stubborn character is obvious, along with his frequent drunkenness.

Herein lay Abigail's struggle. She was trapped in an unhappy marriage to a seeming brute of a man with no possibility of release. Although her husband was wealthy and she would never lack materially, her life circumstances were bleak as far as happiness was concerned. Yet we have much to learn from Abigail's response to her situation.

I will not be concentrating on Abigail's marriage problems. However if you are experiencing abuse of any kind from a marriage partner I urge you to seek urgent help immediately, and find a place of safety.

I've yet to meet the person who has never struggled with something. At its extremity, life has the habit of crashing in around us when we least expect it.

Your struggle will look nothing like mine because the difficulties of life arrive in all kinds of 'packages'. Illness. Disappointment. Betrayal. Unemployment. Grief. Depression. Abandonment. Addiction. Low self-esteem. Pain. Loneliness. Despair. Each one, a package we are unwilling to receive, yet forced by life to open.

A recent Facebook post I read went something like this: I'm fed up with Christians telling me I am exactly where God wants me to be. I don't want to be here. I think acceptance is a 'cop out'? It sounded like one of those packages had just been delivered with her name on it. I didn't know her struggle but I felt her pain. And pain is often worsened when the package is secured by an immovable knot securing a tag marked TRAPPED.

And the one thing that makes the biggest impact on our response is the question of permanence.

Is the situation temporary? Can my sickness be cured? Will I find another job? Can the relationship be mended? If we believe the answer to be 'yes', then our response, no matter the severity of the situation, usually involves being able to see the end of the tunnel. There is still hope.

If, like Abigail, the answer to that question appears to offer a resounding 'no', then altogether different factors come into play. The sickening fog cannot be dispersed by sunshine. We cannot find our way out. We feel trapped. Trapped by the unalterable. Trapped by a pain we believe can never be relieved, a situation that cannot be transformed. And the knot on the package we've been delivered tightens its grip around our heart with a cord of hopelessness.

To make matters worse, it appears that God is finished with us as we allow our circumstances to become our identity.

We are trapped.

Perseverance

Life's circumstances can have a withering effect on our lives. The physical ramifications can be many, whether it's daily dealing with pain, poverty, disability or the like. Yet it's what they do to the heart of our being that has the potential for far greater destruction.

Is fatalism the best way to deal with the agonies we live with? Should we settle with a 'get up and get on with it attitude'? Nothing is going to change so we should just live with it? These are the cards we've been dealt, the life God has given us. Like it or not, we're stuck with it.

Fatalism and acceptance are two different things. Fatalism is passive, a shrugging-of-the-shoulders attitude, wrapped in pessimism. Acceptance is active, a willingness to come to terms with something for positive benefits.

Abigail was no fatalist. She was trapped within a marriage that, humanly speaking, could not be changed. She was in it for the long haul no matter how much she might have wished things to be different. But it is clear by her actions, and the relationship she had with the servants (1 Samuel 25:14ff), that this young woman wanted to make the best of her circumstances. But a positive attitude wasn't Abigail's only reasoning for accepting her lot with Nabal. She had some knowledge of the One True God (1 Samuel 25:26) and she had heard of His protection and His love for the Hebrew nation. She knew of His promise-making and promise-keeping nature (1 Samuel 25:28–29). And, behind her fears, Abigail appeared to believe that her life was bound up in God's plan (1 Samuel 25:30–31).

We are not called to survive by mere fatalism: resigned to whatever horror invades. Passive negativity is not what God wants from us. He wants to bring us to acceptance, with all of its hope for the future; something we not only strive for but also embrace. In the meantime we are called to persevere.

Jesus reminds us not to give up praying against the unacceptable, but urges us to "always pray and never give up" (Luke 18:1 NLT). He goes on to tell the story in verses 2–8 of a widowed lady seeking justice from a judge who wants nothing to do with her case. Eventually it's the woman's persistence that wins through! She wasn't prepared to give in. Jesus hammers home the message that our God is more concerned about His children than an ungodly judge, and that He listens attentively to His children's pleas for justice.

It would be easy to take from this passage that if we continually batter on Heaven's door that God will eventually give us exactly what we are asking for. Bullying God is not the intended lesson! The lesson here is perseverance – don't stop praying. A judicial decision was the right thing for the widow, that's why her persistence was rewarded.

God wants to give us the right thing too. That's why Jesus encourages us to keep bringing our concerns to God. He will answer with what is best for us and for the outworking of His plan. But we won't necessarily get what we want in the way we want it.

Petitioning the Father about personal suffering was exactly what Jesus did. And He did it three times on one particular night. It's heartbreaking to hear Jesus plead for the awful suffering He was about to endure to be removed. He knew it had to happen if the great separation between God and humanity was ever to be bridged. Knew that His suffering, His death, His shed blood, was the only way sin could ever be forgiven. The Son of God knew it had to happen, but the human Jesus pleaded with His Father anyway.

It all ended with deliberate acceptance of God's will: "Nevertheless, not as I will, but as You will" (Matthew 26:39). And Jesus suffered and died.

Fatalism focuses on me.

Acceptance focuses on God's will for me.

Perseverance requires us to set our focus on God.

It is the staying power that helps us to endure until we reach the place Jesus did in the garden where we too can say: *Your will be done, Lord.*

Jesus was able to say those words because His focus was diverted to the bigger, eternal picture: "Who for the joy that was set before Him endured the cross, despising the shame, and is seated at the right hand of the throne of God" (Hebrews 12:2). As far as Jesus was concerned, pleasing the Father by redeeming humankind was worth the suffering.

We also are eternal beings. What happens to us here is about more than now, about more than us: "For our citizenship is in Heaven, from which we also eagerly wait for the Saviour, the Lord Jesus Christ" (Philippians 3:20 NKJV).

But how is it possible to "set your mind on things above, not on the things on the earth," as the Apostle Paul tells the suffering church in Colossians 3:2 (NKJV)? How do we get our head around the eternal when the 'now' is crumbling around us? We need to persevere. To hang on by our fingertips if necessary, all the while remembering that our identity is not found in our circumstances but in our relationship to Jesus Christ. We are children of the King. He will never abandon us – why, *even in the valley of the shadow of death,* He has promised to be with us (Psalm 23:4).

Perseverance requires that we take time to look up from the pain, where He promises "you will seek Me and find Me, when you search for Me with all your heart" (Jeremiah 29:13). Even if the circumstances remain unchanged we start to recognise God's loving presence with us, and the burdens begin to change in appearance...

"... because we know that suffering produces perseverance."
Romans 5:3 (NIV)

Faith

Abigail may have been trapped but she persevered, demonstrating how to live right in spite of all that was going on around her. It is also evident that by directing her focus above her circumstances, her faith in the God of Israel was increased and ultimately rewarded. She was even able to point David, who really shouldn't have needed reminding, of his responsibility to the One who would fight for him (1 Samuel 25:28). Clearly Abigail knew much of the character and power of the Almighty, and sought His will above that of her godless husband.

Faith is a frequently misused word. Faith is not something we ratchet up when we want God to act on our behalf. It's not a concentration of mind and will to produce what we believe needs to happen. There is no such thing as blind faith. God never asks us to take a leap in the dark and hope for the best.

Rather, faith is a reasoned choice we make because we know the One in whom we are trusting. I have faith in my husband when he pushes a chair beneath me as I sit at a table. Why? Because I know him, and I choose to believe that he would not knowingly put a faulty chair below me that might cause me harm. I don't need to examine that piece of furniture for myself when it's already in his hands. More than forty years of marriage have shown that my faith in Philip is justified.

That's the kind of faith that God wants us to have in Him. He wants us to know him in such an intimate way that trusting Him is as natural as breathing.

"Suffering produces perseverance," Paul wrote in Romans 5:3, and perseverance encourages us to shift our focus towards God. But if our vision is blurred, and our circumstances cause us to doubt God's love for us then it is time to pause and look a little closer. Who is this God? What does His character tell me about His heart? How does He see me? Does He really love me… even with all that's troubling me just now?

Amazingly, the answers are readily available to us. God is not hiding from us. Instead He has chosen to reveal Himself to us in a multiplicity of ways. We see Him all around us in His created world. In each dawn which reminds us that darkness always gives way to light. In the repetition of the seasons where spring always follows winter. In the colours of the rainbow splitting a stormy sky, proving that life is not always grey. Creation shows His beauty, speaks His power and reminds us of His faithfulness for "While the earth remains, seedtime and harvest, cold and heat, winter and summer, and day and night shall not cease" (Genesis 8:22).

God also reveals who He is by the images He uses in the Bible to describe Himself as…

- **King of kings** (Revelation 19:16): He is all-powerful. There is none greater.
- **Rock of ages** (Isaiah 26:4): The eternal One. He is always there.
- **Light of the world** (John 8:12): Darkness flees in His presence.
- **Compassionate Father** (Jeremiah 31:3): His love is unchangeable, everlasting.
- **Sovereign Lord** (Jeremiah 29:11): His plans are for our good, not to harm us.

Then there are the names God used to introduce Himself at various times in an individual's extremity, as well as in Israel's difficult history. Names that give us a window to look through, each disclosing a little more of the God who can be trusted…

- **Jehovah Jireh** (Genesis 22:14): The God who provides… all we need.
- **El Roi** (Genesis 16:13): The God who sees… where we are on life's journey.
- **El Shaddai** (Genesis 17:1): The God who is enough… in every situation.

And as we catch a glimpse of who God is, faith begins to rise because we know, even in part, whom we are trusting. And in His powerful hands the chair He places beneath us to seat us at life's shaky table is suddenly secure because we know we can trust Him.

"Faith" – that reasoned choice to trust the God we know – "comes by hearing, and hearing by the word of God" (Romans 10:17 NKJV). God is a speaking God. He wants to speak into our situation. Our part is to open the Book, and we will be thrilled by what we find, for...

"... those who wait on the Lord shall renew their strength; they shall mount up with wings like eagles, they shall run and not be weary, they shall walk and not faint."
Isaiah 40:31 NKJV

Contentment

It's remarkable how Abigail was able to live a contented life under such difficult circumstances. There was no possibility of remission. No change in sight. She continued to look after her home; commanded the respect of her servants; stayed faithful to her churlish husband, and responded wisely to the imminent danger from an invading army. How did she do it?

I believe Abigail had learned the secret of contentment.

The Apostle Paul offers us outstanding guidance on how to be content. He wrote to the Philippian church from the misery of a Roman prison, yet he was able to say: "for I have learned in whatever situation I am to be content. I know how to be brought low, and I know how to abound. In any and every circumstance, I have learned the secret of facing plenty and hunger, abundance and need" (Philippians 4:11–12). Notice that Paul felt it necessary to include finding contentment in the good times as well as the bad. Yet, human nature is such that even when all is well in our lives we want more. It's sad to think that discontentment isn't only the preserve of those facing difficulties.

Despite what you might think, contentment is not equivalent to happiness. Happiness is a feeling dependent on happenings, and they are not always conducive to cheerfulness. Contentment, rather, is a deep satisfaction that can be found in spite of happenings: that sense of peace that attaches itself to acceptance.

Since trusting Christ, Paul was never out of trouble. He was misunderstood, beaten, shipwrecked, imprisoned, homeless, and even abandoned by those he'd called friends. How come he was contented?

What was Paul's secret?

Was he just one of those people we meet from time to time who have such an accepting nature that you think it's been gifted? They never appear to question, never worry and always seem so calm. Oh, how I've wished down the years that I could be like them. But I'm not. That's why I love Paul's secret for contentment.

The secret Paul reveals is not a gift. God hasn't given it to some and withheld it from others. Neither did it happen overnight, as Paul explains in Philippians 4:12. It is something he has learned. Step by step – with every mistake, every trial, every disappointment, and every pain – Paul slowly learned the secret of contentment. And it was nothing to do with his abilities, or the right breaks, or a strong personality. But it had everything to do with developing a deep satisfaction in Jesus.

Each time Paul was knocked down He remembered how he'd been helped previously, and little by little, the apostle discovered that he didn't have to muster up a response to his situation but to rely completely on the strength given to him by Christ. A strength that could not fail – causing Paul's faith in the Saviour to grow, and of whom he eventually said in Philippians 4:13, "I can do all things through Christ who strengthens me."

Trusting God was Paul's secret to contentment. A secret he freely shares with us, for by it we too can know…

- **Peace**, when all around is in turmoil: "and the peace of God, which surpasses all understanding, will guard your hearts and minds in Christ Jesus" (Philippians 4:7).
- **Hope**, when life has none and joy cannot be found: "May the God of hope fill you with all joy and peace in believing, so that by the power of the Holy Spirit you may abound in hope" (Romans 15:13).
- **Purpose**, when nothing makes sense any more: "I want you to know, brethren, that the things which happened to me have actually turned out for the furtherance of the gospel" (Philippians 1:12 NKJV).
- **Reward**, remembering that now is not all there is: "For this light momentary affliction is preparing for us an eternal weight of glory beyond all comparison" (2 Corinthians 4:17).

As with many of life's lessons, there is no magic wand that enables our heart to be at peace. While we are always in a hurry for answers, God is not. It would appear, that apart from salvation that occurs the instant we repent of our sins, trust is something we learn more gradually. God seeks to cultivate deep roots of faith in us that our trust in Him might one day be unshakeable whatever damage life's storms may threaten... even to the point where we can say with Paul: "For to me to live is Christ, and to die is gain" (Philippians 1:21).

Whatever happens, Paul is saying, it is all about Christ. He had learned to take his eyes away from the prison walls that held him and to focus on Christ. That's contentment.

There is little doubt in my mind that Abigail had heard stories of a God who cared enough about His people to rescue them from the Egyptians; provide for them in the wilderness; defeat their enemies and promise them a king who would be "a man after His own heart" (1 Samuel 13:14). It appears it was a simple lesson of memory and mathematics for this woman trapped in a loveless marriage. God's faithfulness was not a 'one day wonder'. Again and again, He meted out His grace. Therefore, she reckoned that if Jehovah could look after Israel's millions, then He could care for her in Nabal's house. Just as Paul would do centuries later, Abigail learned to look to the One who could give her the strength she needed to take her eyes off her circumstances.

And she was content.

It's easy to conclude that Abigail got her fairy-tale ending, but that would be far from the truth. As she rode off into the sunset, it was into a different set of difficulties. Of course David was nothing like Nabal, but she was entering a community on the run. Saul's army was still after David, requiring a nomadic existence for those in the future king's camp. The necessities of life were basic for the more than six hundred people who were to become Abigail's new family. Even food depended on the generosity of locals. Gone was the security of wealth and a solid home to live in. It would be years before Abigail would experience palace life... if indeed she ever did.

But Abigail was no longer trapped – neither by a loveless marriage nor a resentful heart. She had learned to trust in God, and with it had found freedom in contentment.

Trapped: Taking a closer look

For personal or group study

Study questions

1 Read Abigail's story in 1 Samuel 25:1–42. List what encourages, challenges and blesses you from the passage.

2 Do you think Abigail was right to go behind her husband's back to negotiate with David? Use Scripture to back up your response.

3 Why does James say to consider troubles as an opportunity for joy (James 1:2–5)?

4 Using Luke 11:5–9 consider/discuss the importance of persisting in prayer.

5 How can we "set our minds on things that are above" as Paul suggests in Colossians 3:1–4?

6 Read Philippians 4:10–13. Looking back can you identify when and how God has helped you in the past?

7 Would you say you are content in your present circumstances? Take time to identify what you might need to work on, and pray specifically over your struggle.

2
FAILURE
JOHN MARK

I

c. AD 47

"Where are you bound?"

"Seleucia," the sailor replied, barely taking time to glance sideways, heavy sacks shifting on his back as he mounted the steep gangplank.

"Is there a ship bound for Caesarea nearby?" the young man pressed, desperate to get the sailor's attention.

"The *Roma*," he said, tilting his head towards the ship moored a short distance beyond them. "You'd need to hurry, she's lifting anchor."

This was the third ship where John Mark had enquired. He didn't want to miss this chance. If only he hadn't stopped to gather himself on the road from Perga. His heart was beating so quickly after Paul's caustic comments that he took time to rest – no, hide – behind a large boulder on the road from Perga to the harbour at Attalia. He certainly didn't want to go home via Seleucia. It was too close to Antioch. He couldn't face the brethren from the church there. Not after what Paul had said. The apostle's words had cut deep. Played on a loop inside his head. Caused his hands to sweat and his heart to break.

"No one who puts his hand to the plough and looks back is fit for the kingdom of God," were Paul's parting words.

Worse still, the words Paul chose weren't his own – Jesus Himself had spoken them. John Mark remembered Peter telling the church which met in his own home how Jesus had laid out the cost of following him. Discipleship was all or nothing. There was to be no turning back!

But he had to go home. So he raced towards the *Roma*, his mind still running faster than his feet.

He didn't want to let anyone down. Peter, who'd taught him so much. The church at Antioch, who had agreed with Barnabas that he should accompany the two great preachers as their assistant.

Barnabas. Dear, encouraging cousin Barnabas. Humble, generous, always looking out for others. Always looking out for him. Would he ever forgive him for leaving the mission on which the church had sent them? John Mark would certainly never forget the disappointed look on his cousin's face when he announced his departure.

And Mother. His return would surely be an embarrassment to her.

49

Hopefully, she would find it in her heart to welcome him home. Isn't that what mothers were supposed to do?

The *Roma* was about to draw up her gangplank. It could be days or even weeks before he could obtain passage to Caesarea enabling him to bypass Antioch. It was now or never.

"Can you take another passenger?" he hollered to the man he assumed was the captain, as he was shouting orders to "Clear the ship if you're going ashore!"

"Paying passengers only," came the reply.

John Mark rummaged in the leather pouch tied round his waist as he waited for the last of the harbour workers to disembark. Money quickly changed hands and the young man's feet soon landed on the deck.

He was heading home.

Somehow or other, John Mark felt a kind of comfort as he pushed his back between two stacks of sacks resting against the starboard panels of the ship. As the gangplank was raised, and the huge square sail dropped, he found himself surrounded by sailors who didn't know him. Better still, they didn't know he was heading home a failure… reneging on the work to which he'd previously believed God had called him.

And the *Roma* moved slowly from her mooring to the sound of the rising anchor, and to the bellowed orders of a man who'd obviously done this before.

John Mark didn't join the other passengers in viewing the beautiful harbour of Attalia as the merchant ship elegantly made her way out to sea. He was too full of shame and sadness, too busy arguing with himself over the rights and wrongs of his decision to look at scenery. How different that was to when the intrepid threesome first arrived in Asia Minor a short time earlier.

First impressions tend to last. And Attalia certainly didn't disappoint. How different to the smaller harbours of Cyprus. Even Seleucia, with its huge number of ships arriving and leaving daily, was merely a stopping-station compared to the harbour they viewed on arrival in Pamphylia. Its wide entrance welcomed the merchants and travellers of the Mediterranean as a mother would receive her children into her open arms. Mountains to the right and left clothed in verdant forests, she beguiled those who entered with a sense of protection and plenty. But John Mark wasn't fooled. Those same mountains may have provided the Roman army with the best of horses, and many of the surrounding nations with wool and wine, but they were also filled with robbers and disease-ridden insects.

He definitely wouldn't be travelling the Via Sebaste to Antioch in Pisidia. Paul and Barnabas could deal with the robbers and disease without him. He was going home.

The clap of the wind catching the broad sail pulled the young rebel from his thoughts as the *Roma*'s bow dipped into the sparkling blue of the Mediterranean leaving the safety of the harbour behind. Soon the rhythmical movement of the ship combined with exhaustion of both body and soul rocked the dropout to sleep.

II

WHAT?! W-H-E-R-E?

The noise that wakened John Mark so abruptly from sleep seemed to be almost on top of them. Momentarily confused he looked up to discover a black sky pierced with a magnificent array of lights above his head. A cramped bed accounted for the aching of his bones and stiffness of body. He remembered. He was on a ship. A merchant ship. The sacks holding his body upright attested to that fact, providing him with leverage to rise to his feet.

B-O-O-M!

There it was again. A sound louder than thunder yet the sky was clear, the night so quiet it magnified the deafening noise.

B-O-O-M!

This time John Mark felt the *Roma* tilt to port as he tried to steady his feet on deck. Momentarily distracted by a child crying in the only small cabin to the stern, he was almost knocked over by the sailors joining the night watch on deck.

B-O-O-M!

"Trireme to starboard!"

John Mark looked to the boy on the mast shouting the alarm, as he was suddenly thrown to the deck with another sharp turn to port. He crawled back into the tight space he'd pulled himself from a few minutes earlier, knees to his chest, arms covering his head.

B-O-O-M!

Lord Jehovah, I don't want to die! By now the ship was tossing around like the little fishing boats in a storm on Galilee, water splashing over the side soaking him through. *Is this my fault, Lord?* Thoughts of Jonah's disobedience flashed across John Mark's mind as another wave crashed down on him.

B-O-O-M!

Loud shouting interrupted his panic. Sailors started screaming and waving burning torches around him in an attempt to alert the huge three-tier former warship to their presence and position. It was colossal.

Please Lord, let them see us!

B-O-O-M!

Another stroke from the three rows of oarsmen in response to the cox's drumbeat drew a uniform gasp from sailors and passengers alike. Surely the trireme would crash into them? And the *Roma* would no doubt splinter into pieces, consigning them to the bottom of a cold black sea.

Even in the darkness the huge shadow cast by the great vessel covered the small ship as it edged ever closer… but it couldn't hide the disgrace of one man's failure. *Was this how it was all going to end?*

Suddenly, the wake of the trireme hit the stern as the *Roma*'s captain pulled on the wheel, straining every sinew of his portly frame, the assailant's waters pushing the smaller vessel away from calamity. Up and down she plunged in the huge waves, the screams of terrified passengers muted by the noise of both nature and the creaking ship.

B-O-O-M!

This time the drum noise was behind them, the trireme no longer a threat. And the *Roma* gradually steadied as the wake calmed and the water rolled off the deck.

"The gods were with us tonight," John Mark heard one sailor say to another as they inspected the ship's load.

"The One true God rescued us from disaster," John Mark whispered, wringing water from his clothing. "Thank you, Lord," he continued. "I don't deserve Your mercy." If guilt could sink a ship, the *Roma* would already be at the bottom of the ocean.

There was no more sleep on the merchant vessel the remainder of the night – for anyone. It had been a close call.

John Mark's eyes fell on a boy walking the deck after the sun peeked above the horizon. He looked about thirteen. Roman, by the cut of his clothing and hair – and not a poor one at that. But he looked too old to be the child he'd heard crying during last night's near miss. Perhaps he had a sibling? Predictably, the boy drew level with John Mark, his eyes wide with excitement.

"Did you hear the storm last night?" he questioned, following it up quickly with another. "Have you ever heard thunder like that before? It was so exciting."

John Mark guessed a Roman family had the use of the aft cabin, and the children had been led to believe the commotion was a storm.

"It was certainly nothing like anything else I've experienced before," John Mark replied, deciding there was no need to frighten the boy with the actual details.

"Marcus! Marcus!"

A rather frantic looking woman rushed towards the teenager, anxiety written all over her face: "I told you not to leave the cabin! Your pater will be displeased that you've disobeyed me. It's not safe on deck, especially after last night's storm!"

"Mater," the boy replied indignantly, "the sea is calm now. I am just speaking to this gentleman about the storm... please, Sir, tell my mater your name that she might stop fussing?"

"John Mark, Madam."

"We share the same name, Sir," the boy interrupted. "Marcus. My name is also Marcus. Are you Roman? I thought you looked Hebrew, yet you have a Roman name."

John Mark smiled, remembering the exuberance of youth, fuelled by hormones and the desire to appear older than your years.

"My pater is also Roman, young Sir. My mater is Hebrew, hence the Hebrew and Roman names. And my mater taught me the importance of obeying my parents, young Marcus."

The boy turned sullen faced to follow his mother.

"Can you play Knucklebones, John Mark?" he enquired over his shoulder.

"Marcus! Stop bothering the gentleman."

"But Mater, he's safe... he's part Roman."

"Yes, Marcus, I can play Knucklebones, and will give you a game – only with your mater's permission."

The woman sighed. There were more important points to argue over than a game.

"All right Marcus," and while her son pumped the air with his fist, she added, "after breakfast."

Breakfast. The word caused John Mark's stomach to rumble. He hadn't eaten since... well, since before he left Paul and Barnabas in Perga. *Groan.* The lively conversation with Marcus had momentarily paused the guilt he had been feeding on since then. Unfortunately, guilt does nothing to fill an empty belly.

Back in his little alcove, John Mark searched for the knapsack he'd brought on board. It held a little bread and a cake of figs for the long journey home. It was Barnabas who'd pushed the food into his sack. John Mark had been too upset to think about anything but getting away. His search continued without success. He reasoned it had probably washed overboard during the turbulence of the trireme encounter. He'd have to put up with the grumbling of his stomach for many more hours until they reached Caesarea.

"Mater wondered if you'd like to share our breakfast?"

John Mark raised his eyes to see Marcus standing over him, a linen cloth filled with bread and dried fruit in his hands. The runaway couldn't believe his eyes.

"Before they call I will answer," he recited, confusing the boy with his words.

"What?"

"Before I asked the God of Heaven to supply my food you appear with it in your hands!"

"Which god is that?" the boy questioned, barely waiting for a reply. "I should like to know who your favourite god is so that I might add him to the many I already pray to."

"I have no favourite, Marcus, because there is only one God." Marcus almost collapsed on the floor beside him at the thought. "I worship the God who created all things; the God who loves to speak with us – those words I spoke are His, delivered to His people as a promise by the prophet Isaiah many years ago. This great God delights in providing all we need in this life, and for the life to come."

Marcus was speechless for the first time since they'd met, so John Mark continued: "And this God sometimes uses boys like you to do His will. So why don't we eat some of these lovely things."

Marcus was glad to tuck in. This stranger wasn't like anyone he'd met before. His pater had warned them of the strangeness of the Judeans, but believing in only one god was the craziest thing he'd heard. What chance was there of having your prayers answered if you could recite them to only one god? And what if you displeased the god? You'd never have a chance of getting what you wanted. Surely you needed to keep your options open.

During breakfast, John Mark discovered that the Roman family were headed to join Marcus' pater who was senior clerk to the cohort at Caesarea. The boy's chest puffed up proudly when he related how important his pater was, and that he himself would one day be a notable clerk, perhaps even to a senator in Rome. It was good to have dreams, John Mark thought. He silently prayed that the teenager's dreams would not shatter as his had done so shamefully.

The rattle of goat knuckles drew him back from his contemplation. There was a game to play, and John Mark reasoned that Marcus was probably an ace at this game of skill. He wasn't far wrong.

III

Marcus' game plan bordered on cheating, or was at least suspect. The boy's right hand hovered low over the knucklebones on the deck before throwing the one cradled in his left hand into the air. From that position, he had no problem scooping them all up before catching the tossed one again.

"I thought you had to throw, scoop, and catch all with one hand, Marcus?"

John Mark looked a little indignant at the 'new' rules Marcus tried to push on him. Perhaps it was more the embarrassment of being soundly beaten by a thirteen-year-old that grated on him somewhat. But the weary traveller was thankful for the distraction. Concentrating on the smooth white bones of some poor dead goat gave him something else to think about.

The two of them were unexpectedly interrupted by a commotion on the port side and left the game to see what was going on. Marcus wriggled his way through the group to the side of the boat and was rewarded by the sight of a pod of dolphins swimming alongside. And what a display of aerobatics they put on to the applause of both passengers and crew. They appeared to be racing the ship, which was hurried along by a good following wind. Soon they disappeared, no doubt in search of food, and the watching crowd returned to whatever had occupied them previously.

As John Mark turned to go, Marcus called to him: "I see land, John Mark? Are we nearly there?"

John Mark's eyes fell on an island, closer than he thought it should be to the *Roma*, and responded to the boy: "That's Cyprus. We still have a long way to go before we reach Caesarea."

"Have you ever been to Cyprus, Sir?"

John Mark rattled the little bones in his hand as they sat back down on deck. *Does this boy ever stop asking questions?*

"I have, young Sir," John Mark replied. "In fact I left the island a short few weeks ago. Are you ready for another game?"

Marcus' hand reached forward to still John Mark's from shaking the bones.

"I'd rather hear about Cyprus, please," the boy said. "I've never been away from home before now and I want to have plenty of things to tell pater when we see him. Anyway, you're not very good at Knucklebones," he continued, gathering them up in a little linen pouch.

John Mark sighed. He should have sent the boy back to his mater there and then, but perhaps recounting an edited version of one and a half years on Cyprus would be a useful exercise… for both of them.

"Did you live there?" The questions had started. "Were you working there? What is your trade? What is…?"

John Mark raised his hand stopping the boy in full flow.

"Marcus, I set the rules here."

The boy quieted.

"I will tell you about Cyprus and what I was doing there, but if you interrupt me then I will stop and you will return to your cabin. Agreed?"

Marcus nodded, not daring to speak in case his new-found friend followed through on his threat.

"In answer to your question, no, I didn't have a home in Cyprus, I visited the island with friends – although we did stay for one and a half years. In fact, we only left the island a few weeks ago to travel to Pamphylia."

"And…" Marcus' hand shot to his mouth swifter than an arrow in flight. He found it very difficult not to interrupt, but the storyteller could see that at least he was trying.

"My home is in Jerusalem, where I live with my mater, but my cousin Barnabas is from Cyprus so I do have distant relatives there. Myself,

Barnabas, and another man called Saul, sailed from Antioch in Syria to the port of Salamis on a very special mission."

Marcus' eyes widened at the promise of a mystery. Soon he became restless as his new friend explained how the threesome moved from synagogue to synagogue, preaching. It was all a bit boring for the teenager. He knew what a synagogue was – no more than a temple of sorts – to the Hebrew God. He also recognised that religion was important. Everyone needed a 'god' at some time or other, but it was all very far from the story of adventure he thought he was going to hear. He opened his mouth to ask a question but quickly remembered John Mark's threat and closed it again.

"What were you going to ask my young friend?"

Finally, he was allowed to speak.

"I thought you said you were sent to Cyprus on a very special mission, yet you haven't told me who sent you and what was so special about it?"

Marcus shrugged with a look that said if this doesn't get any better I'll go off and play with my little brother.

John Mark saw that he was losing the boy's interest.

"We were sent by the church at Antioch to preach the good news about Jesus to the Jews who live in Cyprus."

"What's a church?" the boy asked. "And who's Jesus?"

"A church is a group of people who meet together to worship God, and especially to learn about His Son Jesus, who died on a Roman cross and rose again from the dead…"

"This Jesus isn't dead anymore?!" Marcus gawped, his chin virtually sitting on his chest. "How? Where is He? That can't be true! When you're dead, you're dead! Don't lie, John Mark!"

"It's true, Marcus," John Mark interjected before the boy could continue. "Jesus is the promised Messiah. He died so that we could be forgiven of our many sins, and He rose from the dead to prove He has power over death, which means that we too will one day rise from the dead to meet Him in God's Heaven."

It all sounded too much like the stories his mater scolded him for telling… the ones he made up to get him out of trouble, or to frighten his little brother. This was one of those crazy stories, except this one was being told by a grown man.

"He can't have been dead, John Mark. He must have been pretending."

"Let me tell you about Jesus, Marcus… about when He was alive."

John Mark started with the story of the boy, about Marcus' age, who'd gone off for the day to find the new rabbi Jesus, hoping he'd see Him perform a miracle. The boy sat with thousands of people on a hillside and Jesus became concerned that they'd be hungry because they'd been listening to Him for so long. The only food Jesus' disciples could find was the lunch the lad's mater had put together for him when he left home. The lad willingly gave it to Jesus, and before you could swing a sling, Jesus had turned it into enough food to feed the whole multitude.

"Over five thousand people, Marcus," John Mark said, "and there were baskets of food left over!"

"From five loaves and two small fish?!" *That was powerful magic* – but Marcus thought better of using that word, as John Mark was calling it a miracle. *At least it was a good story.*

Time sped like the wind as the boy's new friend recounted story after story about the man called Jesus. He held his breath at the one where Jesus was delayed from going to the sick girl whose pater was the synagogue ruler. He was horrified that she had died before Jesus had got to her. But then Jesus went into her room with her parents and, after He spoke to her, she sat up alive!

Then they laughed together at the imagined sight of the friends who broke through a man's roof so they could get their paralysed friend to Jesus. Marcus could hardly believe it. And their ingenuity and persistence saw the man walk out of that home with the broken roof totally healed. The boy hoped he would be that kind of friend one day.

The pair barely noticed lunch arriving as the stories continued. Marcus was fascinated by the One of whom John Mark was speaking as they munched on cheese and bread. But the final story caused the teenager to swipe at a tear. The smiles now gone, John Mark related the story of how his people, the Jews, had handed Jesus over to Marcus' people, the Romans, to crucify the One who had done no wrong. The miracle worker died an excruciating death.

Marcus got to his feet to run back to his mater. He felt overwhelmed. Didn't want John Mark to see him cry. Then he remembered.

"But didn't you say Jesus rose from the dead?"

"I certainly did, young Marcus," John Mark replied, stretching out his hand to encourage him to listen on.

And the boy dropped to the deck again. He wanted – no, needed – to hear the rest of the story.

For the next while nothing could distract the boy from hearing how the tomb was found empty. Even the efficient Roman army couldn't find the body of Jesus.

Where was it? Could Jesus really have come back to life? Was John Mark right? Could the man he'd been hearing about for the past hours actually be the Son of God? The Messiah, as John Mark called Him?

In spite of all the questions racing through his mind, Marcus was really glad to hear that Jesus was alive. This was certainly one story he'd tell his pater. *Maybe Pater knows about Jesus and he will be able to tell me more.*

The silence between man and boy drew Marcus back from his thoughts.

"And this is why you went to Cyprus, John Mark?"

The man nodded, but Marcus saw a sadness spread across his face.

"Why are you going home?" the boy continued. "Does everybody know about Jesus now?"

And the guilt of failure gripped like a vice around John Mark's heart.

IV

The *Roma* cut through the final miles of the journey with precision, her bow dipping sharply into the water as both wind and waves drove her forward. *Roma* could challenge the dolphins easily at this speed, John Mark thought as Marcus responded to his mater's call to come prepare for their arrival. The boy's excitement made him smile. But John Mark wished he could rouse even a morsel of the usual delight associated with homecoming, instead his heart sank still further as a flurry of deckhands busied around him.

As he got to his feet, the returning traveller caught sight of land, and Caesarea in particular, straight ahead. Caesarea was easy to spot with Herod's Palace majestically jutting out into the sea, and the arches of the high aqueduct creating a clever design for the low afternoon sun to play with. Those arriving from Rome for the first time now had good reason to think that Judea wasn't the backwoods they'd been led to believe. The checkerboard streets, massive amphitheatre, and temple to the gods Roma and Caesar Augustus might make them believe that Rome really had taken over the world in every sense. Yet, once they travelled beyond the city they'd discover a different world altogether.

The excitement on deck was at fever pitch. Captain and sailors busied themselves steering the *Roma* into the finest harbour ever constructed. The port was enclosed from storm surges by a concrete block wall. As the "oohs and aahs" of admiration crossed the deck, John Mark couldn't help but wish the admirers remembered what else the master builder Herod the Great was famous for.

Murderer, John Mark muttered under his breath. *Extortioner. Traitor.*

T-r-a-i-t-o-r.

That last word caught in his throat, taking the breath from him. Is that what my brethren will think of me? Am I also a traitor? A traitor to the cause of Christ? Have I let down those who sent me? Have I let down the Saviour? The One who took on the death of the cross for me?

The ship thudded against the dock accompanied by claps of delight from the happy passengers. In no time at all, John Mark was virtually carried down the gangplank by the crowd, but no joy filled his frame as his feet touched terra firma once more.

The dock was buzzing with people meeting family and friends. The sooner he was on the road the better, John Mark thought, when suddenly he felt his cloak almost pulled from his shoulders.

"Pater! Pater! I want you to meet my friend."

Marcus' unmistakable voice interrupted John Mark's determination to find the harbour exit. Reaching to grab his falling cloak, he saw a man in Roman dress being equally manhandled by the teenager. It seemed nothing would do but the two men had to be introduced.

"Marcus," the Roman official said, annoyance vying with pleasure. "Where are your manners?

"Please excuse the boy, Sir, he is overexcited by our reunion."

"But Pater," Marcus continued. "This is John Mark. He sailed with us… and…"

"Greetings, John Mark," the man replied, "I see you have already experienced my son's enthusiasm for conversation."

"Shalom." Both men nodded in acknowledgment of the other. "He reminds me of my youth, Sir," John Mark continued. "My mind couldn't keep up with my mouth either."

Laughter filled the space between, although Marcus was less amused.

"It was a delight to have him speed an otherwise boring journey.

"Goodbye, Marcus," John Mark said, looking the boy directly in the eye. "I hope you enjoy Judea, and I look forward to hearing of your progress as a fine apprentice to your pater in the years to come."

Marcus welled with pride as the two men smiled at the thought, and they parted company. John Mark draped his cloak over one shoulder, not needing it in the heat of the day. Marcus was still talking. It made John Mark smile. As he turned to go, he heard the boy's words to his father: "John Mark told me about his god, Pater. His name is Jesus. Have you heard about him?"

"Oh yes," replied the clerk, his voice barely audible now. "My master Cornelius speaks of him often."

Cornelius!

John Mark could barely contain himself. He was now convinced that Marcus would undoubtedly hear more about Jesus. How was it that God had used him, a failure, to introduce the boy to stories about Jesus and send the same boy into the house of Cornelius?

For the first in what seemed an age John Mark felt a glimmer of hope rise, and a prayer of David fell from his lips as Marcus' words disappeared with the crowd.

"But you, O Lord, are a God who is merciful and gracious, slow to anger, and abounding in steadfast love and faithfulness."

Hearing a few coins rattle in his purse, John Mark headed to the market nearest the town gate, filling his water bottle on the way from fountains ornate with Roman sculpture. Like the man or not, he was glad of Herod's genius in introducing water and sewage facilities into Caesarea. John Mark would have enough water to see him well on his way to Jerusalem. There was only bread to buy and soon he'd leave Caesarea behind. Too many people knew him here.

Waiting beside the gate for a caravan heading south unsettled him. He had already had two close calls with people he knew from the bustling church founded by his friend Philip. They would have given him a place to stay overnight but he couldn't face them. There would be too many questions. Too much embarrassment. As it was, the sun was sinking fast, and so were John Mark's chances of leaving Caesarea before morning. He nibbled at the bread, wrapped his cloak tightly around him, and lay down near to the donkey caravan that would be heading for Joppa early in the morning.

But sleep was not his friend.

Cornelius.

John Mark couldn't get the Roman centurion out of his mind.

It had taken a lot of persuasion for John Mark's mother to give permission for him to travel with Peter and Silvanus. She still regarded John Mark as a boy, in spite of the fact that he had already left his teenage years. To this day, he believed it was Peter himself who coaxed her to let him go. His mother had a soft spot for the big fisherman from Galilee, who had become one of the leaders of The Way. She had often sat at Peter's feet and listened to the stories he told of his three amazing years with Jesus. Day after day, the walls of their home bulged with followers or seekers. There were few who left and never returned, in spite of the growing harassment from the Jewish leaders. They thought Jesus' death would be an end to what they called nonsense, until an empty tomb stared them in the face… to say nothing of what had happened fifty days later on the streets of Jerusalem at Pentecost.

Wrapping his cloak tighter around him against the cold breeze coming off the sea, John Mark's mind filled with thoughts of that journey. Back then, his heart pounded with youthful excitement at every turn. Even the dusty roads passed underfoot without complaint as the young man hung on Peter's every word. The coarse laughter of men close by didn't interrupt his memory of witnessing Aeneas lift his bed from the floor and walk for the first time in eight years! Healed! Right in front of his eyes.

In fact, John Mark was rather surprised that they'd left Lydda so quickly after the miracle, as people were travelling from all around to bring their sick to Peter. But the messengers sent from Joppa had impressed on them to come without delay. The believers had an emergency and they needed Peter to deal with it. By leaving early, they'd managed to cover the eleven miles before the sun was at its height. That was the day John Mark learned an essential lesson. God has no favourites. Kings and… dressmakers… each one important to Him.

What he didn't realise as they headed for Joppa was that the person Peter had been called to see wasn't sick, she was already dead! John Mark thought this person must have been really important to take Peter away from all that had happened at Lydda. Then after six hours of walking, he discovered the disciple at Joppa was none other than a woman… a humble dressmaker. The house was full of widows and orphans, and people this dear lady had helped, each weeping over her loss. The room was like a market stall. Clothing and blankets laid out, covering every space, each a tribute to one so generous. A woman who'd demonstrated her love for Jesus by helping those in need.

Sitting by the gate at Caesarea, the very memory of it after all these years caused a lump to rise in John Mark's throat. *Tabitha.* That was her name. He remembered wondering what the point was in bringing Peter to see a dead woman? It was too late even for Peter to do anything about.

Oh how wrong I was.

He couldn't help but chuckle under the woollen cloak as he recalled the gasps of amazement and tears of joy when Peter walked out of the room minutes later with Tabitha beside him, very much alive and well. Such incredible days! It seemed that miracles followed Peter everywhere, and he – the son of a Roman – was there to witness them.

Peter's influence on John Mark's life birthed a desire in him to give his life wholly to the service of Jesus; to experience for himself what it felt like to heal the sick and preach the good news that Messiah had come.

But it all went so terribly wrong.

And sitting at the gate in Caesarea, waiting to retrace the journey he'd made with Peter almost eight years earlier, John Mark was overwhelmed by the weight of failure. So instead of visiting those churches whose joyful memories had once filled the night hours, he would attempt to avoid them. His shame was too great. How could an assistant of Peter report that he'd left the mission to which the church had commissioned him?

What would Peter say?

John Mark's groans were audible.

The sun had barely touched the night sky when the caravan left for Joppa. Donkeys protested noisily as burdens of wool and linen, perfume, figs, and dried fruits were balanced across their strong backs. Even copper from Cyprus clanged and tinkled as traders set out for the markets of Judea and Samaria with their wares. But John Mark struggled with very mixed emotions.

At least the Via Maris provided a cooling breeze for most of the day. The road was busy with caravans passing in both directions. On the more remote stretches, John Mark felt safe from the gangs of robbers that preyed on lone travellers. The caravan master pushed man and beast hard. He didn't want a night in the open, so they covered more miles than John Mark had expected in just one day, arriving in Joppa with little time to spare before the city gates were closed for the night.

Joppa, well known as a traveller's stopover, had lots of inns where cheap accommodation could be obtained for the night. But John Mark was running short of cash and, for a second night, he chose a piece of hard ground over a bed. He needed to keep those final coins to ensure a travelling place with the caravan for his onward journey.

Yesterday's bread was all but finished as he headed to the nearest well to fill his skin with water. Looking towards the harbour he reckoned that the church would be meeting in Simon's house, now that the work of the day was over. He was missing the gatherings of The Way, and wondered if they'd adopted that strange name given to the believers at Antioch... Christians. He liked the tag that had been given in scorn but was prized by those who delighted to carry with them the name of the Christ.

John Mark recalled two significant things about the man known as Simon the Tanner. Firstly, he smelled awful, yet had the sweetness of Christ in his spirit that helped his guests forget about the permanent odour that attached itself to leather workers. Secondly, it was on Simon's very rooftop that Peter received the vision to go to Cornelius in Caesarea and bring the gospel to Gentiles for the first time.

Simon would give me a bed for the night, he muttered, heading over to bed down next to the donkeys. *Best not,* he thought, pushing his back against an old tree trunk and nibbling on the remaining bread. *Anyway,* he mused, *if today was anything to go by, the caravan master might push hard to reach Jerusalem before dark.* Sleep came easier with exhaustion pulling at his eyelids, while a million gems pierced the inky sky overhead.

After leaving Joppa, it soon became clear that you should never expect donkeys to move at speed. Day one was obviously a fluke and by the time they'd reached Lydda, the poor beasts had had enough. The traveller was starting to become impatient and hungry too. He had rehearsed his homecoming speech over and over again, and if he didn't get to give it soon, he'd head off in the opposite direction and never go back to Jerusalem. But he knew he could never do that. Few might understand his reasons for leaving Paul and Barnabas, even he questioned himself at times, but he had to do the right thing, and own up to his failures... and leave the rest to God.

God.

We've barely spoken since... you know when, Father.

Lydda was a small town at a major crossroads. It was the place where traders and travellers chose which direction they would take to finish their journey. As John Mark observed the comings and goings in the town square, he felt it mirrored his own life at that exact time. He was standing at a crossroads. Each of life's roads pointing in a direction he could travel, but only one was the right one – the one that led to repentance and renewed fellowship with God. Choosing the right one would mean admitting that his failure was his fault. Others might fail because of lack of ability or because of outside forces pressing in, but sitting at the busy junction in Lydda, John Mark knew that those weren't the reasons he was where he shouldn't have been. The dejected saint knew it was time to choose the direction for his soul.

It had been way too long since John Mark had spoken to his Heavenly Father. It was time to put that right.

Our Father in heaven, hallowed be your name.

There seemed no better prayer to pray than the one Jesus taught the disciples. the words reminding John Mark to whom he was actually praying. There was none greater.

Your kingdom come, your will be done, on earth as it is in heaven.

As the words left his mouth, the petitioner recognised he was asking for whatever was left of God's will. The threesome had left Antioch as part of the mission to see God's kingdom come, and they'd set out in God's will. He gulped deeply before he could continue.

And forgive us our debts, as we have forgiven our debtors.

John Mark didn't need others to list his debt of sin. He could do that all by himself. But could he forgive those who had sinned against him? The faces that formed behind his eyelids were of those the prayer prompted him to forgive. How could he do less when he was asking God to forgive him? He was no better than they. Words of forgiveness and repentance flowed as freely as the tears that made tracks down his dusty cheeks. And with them he felt the presence of Heaven for the first time since he'd left Perga.

He was forgiven.

And lead us not into temptation, but deliver us from evil.

John Mark would need to call on all the power of Heaven to complete his journey… and he wasn't thinking only of the road to Jerusalem.

Amen.

The ancient word sealed his oath. There was no going back now.

V

c. AD 67

Passing the State Agora speedily, John Mark had no time to engage in his usual pleasantries with the stallholders. There would be no friendly banter over prices with the spice merchant today. Instead, he waved his greetings as his feet moved faster than would normally be deemed appropriate for a middle-aged man. Across the tiled pavements of the upper city he hurried, past the marbled homes of wealthy Roman businessmen stretching up the hillside on both sides of this gateway to Asia Minor. By the time John Mark puffed through the arch leading into the lower city, the youthful curly-topped messenger was only visible in the distance.

"Timothy says you've to come quickly. A letter has arrived from Paul," the youngster had reported, leaving as quickly as he'd arrived.

A letter from Paul!

John Mark's heart was pounding from more than the exertion. Letters from Paul brought such excitement to the church at Ephesus. Hadn't he been in Rome seven years ago when Paul wrote his letters to the churches with whom he now lived and worked? Back then he couldn't believe his ears when Paul encouraged the church at Colossae to welcome him, should he ever visit. He had discovered first-hand that letters from Paul were transformational in more ways than one. Especially to someone with his history.

Theatre Street was buzzing as usual as he pushed past those bartering for goods in the Agora where the less wealthy shopped. However, he was glad that Demetrius the silversmith was busy enough not to notice him pass by. Feelings still ran high against the Christians among those whose livelihoods depended on selling idols and related bric-a-brac.

Priscilla and Aquila's business was just ahead within the shadow of the amphitheatre. Even those recently arrived in Ephesus knew of the near riot that led to Paul's flight from the city years earlier. As John Mark approached the tentmakers' stall, he recognised some of the other believers heading in the same direction. The air was thick with anticipation as they made their way around the back to Priscilla and Aquila's home, where the church met.

Quick foot washing, carried out by some of the younger believers, welcomed those who'd gathered while, in their usual manner, Priscilla and Aquila warmly greeted each one in turn. John Mark loved the heart this pair displayed to both seeker and saint alike. The church at Ephesus owed much to the devoted couple.

Ephesus' young pastor, Timothy, appeared engrossed in the pile of parchment sitting on the table in front of him. Paul's faithful deliveryman, Tychicus, stood slightly to Timothy's left as John Mark settled against the wall. Paul's letters had a tendency to be long so he felt the need for a little support to help him listen closely.

"Brothers and sisters."

Aquila was on his feet bringing the company to order.

"Silence, please, as we pray before Pastor Timothy brings us news from our beloved Paul."

Even the children bowed reverentially while the Spirit was implored for wisdom and understanding to be given to all who had gathered.

"This is not a letter for the church."

Timothy's opening remarks brought a spread of curiosity across many faces, leaving John Mark wondering what was going on.

"It's a personal letter from my spiritual father," Timothy continued, a slight shake in his voice. "Paul wrote this letter, which Tychicus has carried all the way from Rome, that I might have one final correspondence from him."

A communal gasp seemed to suck the air out of the room.

Final! Was Paul dead?

John Mark wished Timothy would speak faster...

"But I felt it was important for the church to hear the main contents, as they will be of benefit to you as well as me."

The next few hours seemed to pass in a flash as Timothy slowly and carefully read Paul's words, even taking time to repeat some of the contents. The letter contained words of thanksgiving for the young man's faithful service, a call to endure even through periods of inevitable suffering, challenge to beware of false teachers, encouragement to pursue godliness and hold fast to the Scriptures, a reminder to remember always what Jesus Christ had endured for us, and an appeal to preach the Word whatever else was going on.

The room was filled with an unfamiliar silence. The usual interruptions for Timothy, Aquila, and Priscilla to explain what Paul was saying were eaten up in a sadness John Mark hadn't felt in the church before. It was almost as if the congregation was giving a dying man one last uninterrupted opportunity to speak to them.

"For I am already being poured out as a drink offering," Paul wrote, "and the time of my departure has come."

Sobs pierced the silence like the first stars of the night.

"I have fought the good fight, I have finished the race, I have kept the faith."

Few could say that as truthfully as Paul, John Mark thought as Timothy tried to raise the mood by quoting Paul's addition of all that lay ahead for him after death, as well as for all those who love the Saviour.

"Paul has asked me to come to him as quickly as I can," Timothy told his congregation. "Before winter, if possible," he concluded, his voice trembling. "I don't know if I will be too late, but I shall try."

The mood was subdued when Timothy brought the gathering to a close, advising them to go home and to think about what Paul had written. On this occasion, discussion could wait until the next time they met.

John Mark's heart was heavy as he rose to leave, barely hearing Timothy call his name as the crowd dispersed. Joining with a few others whom the young pastor had asked to stay, he listened carefully to the more private parts of the letter that Timothy had decided were too personal to read to the whole church. They contained Paul's final greetings to his fellow workers, and much-loved companions. Specifically, there were special words to Priscilla, Aquila, and Onesiphorus, and a message to the man who had let Paul down a long time ago.

"Get Mark and bring him with you," Timothy read, his eyes sympathetically fixed on his friend, "for he is very useful to me for ministry."

John Mark gasped...

Two decades after he had deserted the great apostle, Paul was sending for him. It was difficult to take in. *Paul asking for me?!* And as the ground swayed beneath his feet and his shoulders shook, John Mark felt the comforting hands of those who could only guess at what this meant to the man who had often felt the ghost of failure cast its dark shadow over his life.

They could never understand.

Never understand the shame of what he'd done. Never understand what it was like to walk away from God's calling on his life. Never understand the anguish of that journey home: what it was like to be looked on as a failure, a traitor even. Neither could those friends surrounding him now ever comprehend the pain of accusations made behind his back. Nor could they understand what it was like to experience guilt rise regularly in his throat like bile after tainted fish.

Except for one person.

There was one who did understand. One who loved him in spite of his mistake. One who had personally experienced the sleepless nights, endured the shame, and was only too aware of the corrosive destruction of unremitting remorse. Whose failure had been weighed in the scales of man's judgment as worse even than his.

Peter.

Peter, who had played with him as a lad, treated him like a son, taught him the gospel of Christ, prayed with him and for him. He it was who had been key in his recovery.

Cousin Barnabas, ever the encourager, had been the one to give him a second chance even when Paul had said "no". Barnabas had chosen him over going with Paul; he had accepted his apology, believed his remorse, and had taken him back to Cyprus a second time. Barnabas had always done everything right, but Peter alone knew the turmoil in John Mark's heart: the constant fear of messing up again. Wasn't that why John Mark had sought him out after Barnabas died in Cyprus?

Barnabas may have given him a second chance, but Peter taught him that God doesn't simply hand out opportunities for us to do it better a second time round. He explained to him that God is a God of restoration. He forgives those who've messed up, makes new the failure, and gives enabling power to complete the tasks He gives us. If John Mark hadn't learned that lesson, he would never have become Peter's interpreter, assistant, fellow worker and trusted writer of all that Peter had seen and learned when he had personally walked with Jesus. That wasn't just a second chance. It was a new start in life!

But more importantly, Peter would have understood what those words from Paul really meant to John Mark: "Get Mark and bring him with you." Hadn't Peter heard something similar after betraying and deserting the Lord?

"But go, tell his disciples, and Peter..." the angel said to the women who had discovered Jesus' empty tomb on resurrection morning.

And Peter...

John Mark remembered how the tears still rolled down Peter's cheeks into his beard when he related the incident years later. What was it his mentor had told him? *When the angel mentioned my name, I dared to believe that Jesus had forgiven me, even if others hadn't... even if it took years for me to forgive myself.*

Get Mark...

Paul had forgiven him. Perhaps it was time to forgive himself?

Timothy was still talking when John Mark returned from his reverie... something about a cloak at Troas and parchments.

"What do you say, John Mark? Will you come with me?"

Those were words he didn't need to hear a second time. He was out the door to pack before Timothy even mentioned when they'd be leaving. And as he hurried past the spice-merchant again he heard him call out: "What? No conversation today John Mark? Where are you off to in such a hurry?"

"Rome, my friend!" he shouted back. "God is sending me to Rome. I must hurry!"

The spice merchant shook his head and smiled. "God is sending him to Rome... Whatever next?"

And John Mark felt his heart lighter than it had been for a very long time, as the cloak of failure slipped from his shoulders.

Adapted from the story of John Mark as found in:

- Acts 12:12, 25; 13:1–3; 15:36–40
- Colossians 4:7–10
- Philemon verse 24
- 2 Timothy 4

Failure: Life lessons

The struggle

Failure is universal.

It started way back in the Garden of Eden when Adam and Eve failed to follow God's simple instructions. They became less than God asked of them through disobedience. Their failure was catastrophic personally, as well as for their future family, to say nothing for life on earth from that point on.

The possibility of failure is as consistent as life itself. Yet, conversely, built within the human psyche is the desire to succeed – or perhaps it's more to do with being *seen* as successful. It seems that no one wants to be viewed as a failure, either by themselves or, more importantly, by others. To be less than expected, or not to achieve what was initially predicted or asked of you, can produce within us a destructive negativity.

Failure has the potential to exert such power over our lives that Emily Owen in her book, *God's Calling Cards,* questions whether everything we do now is overshadowed by past failings?[1]

However, the influence failure produces comes in various degrees. The fact that I've failed miserably at baking pavlova doesn't particularly affect my life in a significant way. I'm quite happy to leave that particular skill to others. Unfortunately, the same can't be said about other personal failures, where sleepless nights and tears have resulted, denting confidence and producing lingering shadows that adversely impact the here and now, and even the future.

While it can be unhelpful to overthink where and how we've gone wrong, identifying the underlying cause helps to ready our hearts for moving forward. To do that we need to ask the question, "How did I get here?" The answer may very well point us towards the remedy. Was it…

- **Lack of ability**, or gifting, for the task at hand? Could it simply be that I was the wrong person for the job? We each have very different skills. That doesn't mean we shouldn't ever step out of our comfort zone, but it might mean we have to train, or try a number of times, before we get it right.

- **External pressure**, or opposition? Failure is not always our fault. Life events such as sickness, disability, bereavement, persecution, and opposition may bring to an end what seemed so right when we first started out. Success may appear to be within reach but can subsequently crumble under external pressure.

  Yet it is important to remember that such pressures do not occur in a vacuum. God is in control of our lives and is more than aware of our circumstances. Remember that "thorn in the flesh" Paul speaks of in 2 Corinthians 12:7–9? This particular situation led the great apostle to recognise that his successes were all to do with God's power rather than his personal ability.

- **Sin/disobedience?** How often the path to failure is covered by the tarmacadam of selfish desire. I'll do this, or go there, but it has to be done my way, in my time, and under my terms. This is surely a recipe set for disaster.

Yet rarely is there only one cause.

Unfortunately, we are not told why John Mark turned back from the church's commission to accompany Paul and Barnabas on what became known as Paul's First Missionary Journey. Many others would have jumped at the chance of travelling as assistant to these great men of faith. And, at first, that's exactly what John Mark did, for a full year and a half. But suddenly, and just when things appeared to be getting really exciting, their young assistant left them high and dry (Acts 13:13–14). Little comment is made at this stage in Scripture, but later Paul and Barnabas split over John Mark's actions. Paul was unable to hide his displeasure at John Mark's behaviour (Acts 15:36–41).

There has been much speculation over why John Mark failed to stay the course, from family circumstances to spiritual immaturity. But the truth is we simply do not know. What we do know is that it had a detrimental effect on John Mark, and caused dispute between two great missionaries of the early church.

To all intents and purposes, John Mark's early life was one big training ground for a life of Christian service. Standing on the edge looking in, it would have been easy to peg him for the next big job in the early church. From a purely secular stance, he came from a good family, had a great education, and the availability of funds to finance travelling. Yet it was his spiritual background that marked him out. It is thought that it may have been in John Mark's home where Jesus and His disciples shared the Last Supper. That the family's large upper room was the place where the disciples and followers of Jesus hid after the crucifixion, and where Jesus appeared to them following the resurrection. The very place where the promised Holy Spirit came in power upon those gathered.

Up until this time, John Mark was looking on from the sidelines as a boy, while privileged to grow up in the house at the centre of the church's birth. Imagine the discussions heard at his dinner table. Picture the guests he met at his home. There was no more exciting place in the whole of Jerusalem to be brought up. It was not hard to become a follower of The Way when literally surrounded by all the evidence you'd ever need to believe, from the very people who had personally walked with Jesus.

Surely this was one man set for success.

Yet, sadly, nothing could be further from the truth. John Mark messed up. In spite of his spiritual privilege, the ladder to success came tumbling down, injuring more than his reputation. He would never hold a position of leadership. He would always be the assistant from here on in. But what he learned along the way blessed not only the church in his day, but also provided the world with the Gospel of Mark, thus introducing Jesus to millions of people.

Yes, John Mark's struggle was failure, but his mistake helps us realise that while it is human to fail, we should not embrace it as an identity, but rather a place of transition and learning.

While all of us have past situations we'd love to return to and change if we could, yesterday is now beyond our reach. But today is ours in which to make the right choices with God's help, and tomorrow is part of the divine plan for us to follow in true success.

Remember, "Failures are fatal only if we fail to learn from them".[2]

Failing successfully

Was life always this intense?

Is the mantra to 'make something of your life' really the best message we can give to our young people, or espouse for ourselves? These words make an immediate assumption that what or where we are is not good enough. Whether it's to look better, earn more, achieve more, or attain recognition, we are told to work harder, smarter, and faster if we are to be successful.

But what is success? Which image of a successful life is the one we aspire to?

It certainly appears that the answer to that question involves the attainment of wealth, health, and happiness. If any, or all three, of these are missing then the cloud of failure hangs over our lives. Add in a specific goal that has had results less than expected or desired, then that dark cloud is sure to burst over our dreams.

There's one huge problem with this mindset… it portrays a false picture of success. It encourages us to join a rat race that continually asks more of us, reminding us that we are only as good as our latest achievement. It feeds us lies that destroy joy and contentment, while never quite presenting us with the security we long for. In essence, we settle for a second-best existence that we may not even recognise as such, if it were not for the sense of dissatisfaction in our soul.

The Bible makes it clear that God does not measure success by achievements, busy lives, or how far out front we are in the rat race. His measuring stick for success is marked by the depth of our dependence on Him, and our contentment with the plans He has for us. That's why it is absolutely possible to fail successfully – two words you would not normally put together. In God's economy failure that results in a closer spiritual walk with Him is spelled S-U-C-C-E-S-S. The only downside is it frequently means we've arrived there by a more circuitous route via difficult circumstances, bad advice, or worse still, a stubborn heart. It's sad that we often learn the hard way.

So, how do you fail successfully?

Paul gives us expert advice on that very thing. In spite of being in prison, something that was deemed only for those of despicable character and lawless ways, the apostle demonstrated that the appearance of failure was something God could use in positive, powerful ways.

"I want you to know, brothers," he wrote to the church at Philippi, "that what has happened to me has really served to advance the gospel" (Philippians 1:12).

What had happened to Paul? His freedom had been taken from him. He was imprisoned in Rome; now identified with thieves, murderers, and the disreputable. How could the gospel be advanced while he was sitting in death row awaiting execution? Had Paul's mission to reach the world with the good news of Jesus Christ failed? Was the success of his great missionary journeys sullied by his degrading circumstances? Some might say yes, and many of his followers did desert him (2 Timothy 4:10, 14, 16), but Paul went on to clarify to the Philippians why his "failure" was in fact success.

". . . it has become known throughout the whole imperial guard and to all the rest that my imprisonment is for Christ," he explained. "And most of the brothers, having become confident in the Lord by my imprisonment, are much more bold to speak the word without fear" (Philippians 1:13–14).

What resulted from years in prison was that Paul's mission didn't stop because of where he was. Instead, Christ was preached to men – hardened soldiers, in fact – who may never have heard of God's love for them if His messenger had not been under arrest. Success! And young believers were strengthened in their faith by observing, up close and personal, how the godly live when life is tough. No sermon could have taught them as much. Success!

It may have been something the apostle had to point out in his letter to the Philippians, as there were those who saw his imprisonment as disgraceful, but it was a show-and-tell lesson they'd never forget. This was a lesson in success, not failure.

I'm sure that in the mission planning rooms of Jerusalem and Antioch, the idea of spending valuable preaching time in prison would not have been included in their instruction advice for successful ministry. But then Isaiah 55:8 makes it clear that God's thoughts differ from ours, as do our ways from His. And learning to think like Him, and see the world as He does, is the very place where success and failure are often turned on their heads.

Instead of chasing selfish dreams and human accolades which lead to dissatisfaction and an insatiable desire for more, Christ Himself tells us to: "seek first the kingdom of God and his righteousness, and all these things will be added to you" (Matthew 6:33). The Saviour encourages us to turn our worldview upside down. His message is not to look after 'number one', or even make yourself 'number one', but rather to decide to make God, His kingdom, and His righteousness first in your life. When we set the most important pieces of life's puzzle in their proper place, the rest fits together beautifully – and, one day, the picture will be complete.

It's clear that John Mark's failure in ministry was turned on its head, as a few short years later we see him return to Cyprus with cousin Barnabas. Because of this, the successful missionary duo went their separate ways (Acts 15:36–40), Barnabas taking John Mark with him to Cyprus, and Paul taking Silas as his assistant to Syria and Cilicia. Yet even in this failure of trust and communication, God's work was doubled rather than hindered, as two teams now journeyed with the good news instead of just one.

We're not told what led to John Mark's repentance but it can certainly only have happened after his priorities fell in line with Jesus' commands in Matthew 6:33. From that point on it would be God, His kingdom, and His righteousness that would take first place in the young man's life.

The well-worn saying 'failure is not final' was visible in John Mark's life, even if it did take some people a long time to see it. I wonder how long it took for John Mark to believe it for himself?

Biblical success

I'm sure John Mark had biblical heroes. After all he was brought up to know the Jewish Scriptures. As a boy did he and his friends act out the stories of Moses delivering God's people from Egypt, or David downing the giant Goliath with a slingshot? Was the great general Joshua his 'superman', or did the sight of Elijah defeating the prophets of Baal fill his daydreams?

Yet I can't help but wonder how old John Mark was before he discovered that his heroes had failings too? Did he know of Moses' reluctance to follow God's call to return to Egypt? Did David's shameful adultery with Bathsheba and the ensuing death of her husband Uriah, ever cast a shadow over his boyhood admiration for Israel's great king? Was the boy John Mark even aware that Joshua's arrogance at Ai lost them the battle, or that Elijah ran away when a woman threatened him?

With all that was going on in Jerusalem in his teenage years, John Mark's list of heroes would have grown longer as he met with those who had witnessed the miracles of Jesus. Maybe had even been involved in them. Undoubtedly, Simon Peter would have been among them. After all he was the man who had walked on water. He was Jesus' right-hand man.

But by this time, John Mark also knew that Simon Peter was the same man who had denied Jesus with oaths and curses. The man who left Jesus alone in His darkest hour.

Simon Peter was the man who ran away.

Just like he had!

Amazingly, God teaches us more through failure than through apparent success. I have no doubt that John Mark learned much about dealing with failure from Peter. He would have been taught about humility and repentance, as well as God's loving concern for His children – even when they get it wrong. On their many travels together, John Mark would have heard Peter relate those words spoken to him by Jesus, later recorded in Luke 22:32, "Simon, Simon… I have prayed for you that your faith may not fail." Jesus had prayed to the Father for the man who would let Him down.

The Saviour knew that Peter's failure would be monumental but in the days to follow He also knew His words would bring encouragement to the fisherman's shame-filled heart. He reminded the fisherman that his failure wasn't the end. "And when you have turned again," Jesus told him, "strengthen your brothers" (Luke 22:32). It took a walk along the beach with Jesus after the resurrection before Peter believed that he was forgiven, before he realised that God wasn't finished with him yet. Jesus' words, "Feed My sheep" (John 21:17), to the man who'd abandoned Him echoed those He had spoken earlier "strengthen your brothers" (Luke 22:32).

Not once had Jesus used a wagging finger of accusation with Peter. Instead, the Saviour gave the man with the big heart the same number of opportunities to declare his love and commitment as times he had denied Him. Three times Peter had denied the Lord. Three times Jesus asked Peter if he loved Him. Three times the repentant failure replied in the affirmative.

"Lord, you know everything; you know that I love you," Peter wisely replied to the thrice searching question of the Master (John 21:17). Then "Follow Me," Jesus said to Peter (John 21:19). "Stop concerning yourself with other people and do what I ask of you. You follow Me" (my paraphrase of John 21:21–22).

And the rest is history. Peter didn't dwell on his failure. From that moment on he followed Jesus, and discovered that true success was depending on the One who had forgiven him – and given him a second chance.

Peter and John Mark came to accept that past failings do not define us. Rather, if offered to God, our failure is used as a springboard to true success – dependence on God. The Bible never hides the failures of the men and women within its pages. Instead, it honestly displays human frailty and sinfulness that we might be all the more aware of where true strength comes from. It demonstrates what success actually looks like when placed beyond the selfish ambition of humanity into the realm of godliness set against a backdrop of eternity.

Although King David's adultery was always the tarnish on his glittering reign, when he was dying he didn't boast to his son Solomon of his successes. Instead, he instructed Israel's next king to "keep the charge of the LORD your God, walking in his ways and keeping his statutes ... that you may prosper in all that you do and wherever you turn" (1 Kings 2:3). Success, Solomon, is doing things God's way!

The road back

At the start of this section, we thought on the cause of failure and concluded that it is often perceived when external circumstances come into play. Lack of the required skills, health issues, personal and family emergencies, as well as the actions of others, can lead to a change in life's direction that we might see as failure. They may indeed be temporary, and with the needed help and time we find ourselves involved once again in the situations that previously had to be abandoned.

However, it may also be the case that we have to let go of our plans and dreams in order to walk the path God has for us, even if humanly speaking it holds less than we desire. God has a way of stepping into what seems like a straight road to success in order that we learn to depend on Him, rather than ourselves. Ask Job!

Personally, in our own lives, we thought we had it all figured out. We weren't out for the acclaim of others or monetary gain. My husband and I loved God, and had set out on a course of study and training that would lead us to the foreign mission field. Two years into our marriage, we discovered that God had other plans. When our first child was born with multiple disabilities, our dreams shattered. The straight road to successful service suddenly had a bend in it that we couldn't see around. There would be no far flung mission for us. Apart from the deep personal pain we were going through, God took us on a journey that resulted not in what we had to offer Him, but of learning what faith in God really looked like. Of discovering that total dependence on God wasn't weakness or failure, but rather, true success. And our hearts and lives were moulded by acceptance – acceptance that God knew what He was doing even if we didn't.

Those difficult years taught us that not reaching the foreign mission field was not a failure, but a bowing to God's sovereign will. It's an unfinished journey, as God is in the business of *conforming* us to the image of His Son (Romans 8:29). He wants us to become like Jesus, whatever it takes.

There are two responses on our part that help to change how we see our circumstances, and enable us to leave the resultant negativity and feelings of failure behind.

- **Acceptance:** Too often we fight against the circumstances that have scuppered our plans, rather than seeking God for His wisdom on the situation. I discovered the hard way that this approach is wasted energy – energy that we need if we are to move forward through the difficult times. I'm not speaking of fatalism here, but acceptance. As we learned from Abigail, fatalism is a passive resignation that nothing can be changed. It's a negativity that says we're stuck with our lot. Acceptance on the other hand is recognition of God's hand in the situation, which in turn fuels a willingness to trust, which ultimately brings peace, and restores contentment.

  "And we know that for those who love God all things work together for good, for those who are called according to his purpose."
  Romans 8:28

- **Forgiveness:** It's a human trait to look for someone else to blame when things go wrong, even if it's not always the full story. But there are occasions when the actions of others impact us in ways that change the trajectory of our lives. And, apart from having to deal with the fallout of another's actions, we waste time and effort accusing others, which can lead to bitterness, and even hatred. Before we know it "'the root of bitterness' springs up and causes trouble," we're told in Hebrews 12:15, "and by it many become defiled". Bitterness is bad news with a capital 'B'!

Only one course of action can produce the needed change. Forgiveness. We need to forgive the person who has wronged us and let God deal with the destructive root burrowing its way in our heart. It's not easy – but no one ever said following God would be easy. It's especially difficult if the person involved isn't seeking forgiveness, or refuses to accept any wrongdoing.

Jesus never forgave the unrepentant, so while Matthew 5:44 encourages us to "love your enemies and pray for those who persecute you," forgiveness is more to do with releasing us from the wrongdoer's clutches than of seeing their sin purged. That's something they need to repent of for themselves. "When we forgive," I once read on a poster, "we set a prisoner free, only to discover that prisoner is me!"

You may think that forgiveness is a big thing to ask of yourself, but the rewards are transformative.

John Mark went on to achieve great things in missionary service. He returned to Antioch and Cyprus with Barnabas, yet it's the rift between Paul and Barnabas that is remembered. After Barnabas died, it's believed that John Mark travelled extensively with Peter, acting as his assistant and translator, yet there are few accounts available for us to examine. He went on to author the Gospel of Mark, yet it's a surprise to many of us to discover it was **this** John Mark who did so. Church historians provide evidence that the same man was greatly used in founding the flourishing church in Alexandria, Egypt, yet the Bible is silent about it. And although Paul specifically sends for John Mark before his death, stating that he is "very useful for me for ministry" (2 Timothy 4:11), it's more likely that we remember him as the young apprentice who left Paul and Barnabas in the middle of their first missionary journey.

Why is it that we find it so hard to forget the failings of others?

And why do we allow our own failures to pin us down in such a way that any forward movement is rendered impossible? Regret is good. Failure should make us sad. But it's not enough. Wallowing in self-pity won't do it for us either, as we learn from those in Scripture who made a mess of things.

- **Moses** finally trusted God and led the Hebrews out of slavery in Egypt. Check out the book of Exodus for yourself.

- **Joshua** dealt with the sin in the camp as God instructed, and then, depending on God rather than his own military skills, returned to Ai and won the battle (Joshua 7).
- **David,** after attempting to cover his sin with Bathsheba, repented with great remorse (2 Samuel 12:13; Psalm 51), and went on to rule Israel in humility and under God's guidance. Speaking centuries later, the Apostle Paul reminds us that God spoke of David as "a man after my own heart" (Acts 13:22). How come? The answer is found in the same verse as God says: he will do everything I want him to do.

Those three are just a few of the men and women we read about in Scripture who got it wrong but then went on to get it right. Each one had to learn the lesson. God isn't interested in the successes measured by this world's standards. To be wealthy no more proves success than poverty proves failure. God isn't impressed by our achievements, or even by our sacrifice. His interest lies in our dependence on Him.

While independence shouts, "I don't need God", dependence teaches us about God's greatness, His unlimited love for us, His deep care over us, His unchanging faithfulness, and His grace towards us (Lamentations 3:22–23). Dependence also reflects Paul's words in Philippians 4:13 (NLT), "I can do everything through Christ, who gives me strength." So instead of thinking you need to hold the world together all by yourself, hand it over to the One who made it in the first place.

Failure's greatest success is recognising that God's way is best. It can be a spiritual springboard to a healthy dependence on God.

Our discussion on acceptance and forgiveness is just as relevant in personal failure as that caused by circumstances that are out of our control. However, there are additional steps that will prove helpful as we journey forward.

- **Retracing our steps:** Joshua returned to Ai. John Mark went back to Cyprus. Our consideration of where we went wrong will probably not involve a physical journey but it will be a useful spiritual exercise, nevertheless. Was it selfishness? Pride? A longing for recognition? Money? The desire for personal comfort? Disobedience? Whatever the firing pin for our actions, it's good to identify the starting point before we can usefully progress to…

- **Repentance**: How wonderful it is to know that: "If we confess our sins, He is faithful and just to forgive us our sins, and to cleanse us from all unrighteousness" (1 John 1:9).

- **Restoration:** Change does not come overnight. Repairing and rebuilding can take time, especially as restoration is centred on mending our relationship with God. It's what He does in us that is important, and where our heart should be focused from this moment on.

- **Trusting Christ with our weakness:** He uses our weakness to demonstrate His power: "My grace is sufficient for you," God tells us, "for my power is made perfect in weakness" (2 Corinthians 12:9). Paul understood this oxymoron so completely that he was able to follow those words with, "For the sake of Christ, then, I am content with weaknesses, insults, hardships, persecutions, and calamities. For when I am weak, then I am strong" (2 Corinthians 12:10). Content with weaknesses? This is only possible when we trust them to Christ who will turn them around and do something powerful with them.

- **Acquiring a different mindset:** Stop judging your life by human achievement. Instead, "Don't copy the behaviour and customs of this world, but let God transform you into a new person by changing the way you think. Then you will learn to know God's will for you, which is good and pleasing and perfect" (Romans 12:2 NLT). Ask God to help you see things from an eternal perspective. To align your heart for others with His.

- **Developing a servant's heart:** One of the key themes in Mark's Gospel is that of the servant heart of Jesus. When the brothers James and John asked Jesus for a place of honour when He came into His kingdom, Jesus instructs the disciples not to seek to "lord it over" (Mark 10:42) others, but rather, "whoever would be great among you must be your servant" (Mark 10:43). They, and we, are to have lives marked by humble service. The same service that Jesus displayed throughout His ministry reminding them, "even the Son of Man came not to be served but to serve, and to give his life as a ransom for many" (Mark 10:45). John Mark took this teaching to heart. He never became a frontman. He was always the one working for others in the background. I guess his earlier failure in ministry taught him a great deal. He learned to depend on God rather than his own ability. To trust the Faithful One for his everyday needs. To seek God's guidance for a life after failure.

To ignore the opinions of others. But ultimately, restoration in his life revealed itself in selfless service, a trait pleasing to God.

"… so we speak, not to please man,
but to please God who tests our hearts."
1 Thessalonians 2:4

Failure: Taking a closer look

For personal or group study

Study questions

1 What did the Apostle Paul learn about God and about himself from the thorn in the flesh he writes about in 2 Corinthians 12:7–10?

2 Many of God's promises are conditional. God works with us. What is the condition attached to God's promise in Psalm 37:23–24 for those who have failed?

3 Examine the emotions that surface as you explore the subject of God's sovereignty in Job 12. How important is the acceptance of these things in moving forward? Can you echo Job's response in Job 19:25–26?

4 Forgiving those who have wronged us is a big ask. Investigate Jesus' teaching in Matthew 5:44, 6:14–15, 18:21–22. Seek God's strength for whatever He is asking of you.

5 Psalm 51 is a deeply personal prayer of repentance. Using this psalm discuss what real repentance looks like. Might you need to use it today?

6 How would you rate yourself? Independent or dependent? In what ways does that need to change? Use Proverbs 3:5–6 to see how you fare.

7 Meditate on what a servant heart looks like in John 13:1–17.

3

SPOILED
THE WOMAN OF
SAMARIA

I

c. AD 29

"Only fools and buzzards venture out at this time of the day!"

Nathanael's remark echoed the thoughts of the tired men tramping the winding path to Sychar, the silhouette of a buzzard an unwelcome sight overhead. Philip stopped briefly to shake a stone from his sandal and to add to his friend's grumbling.

"And only fools and buzzards trample through this ungodly territory."

"We should have crossed to the other side of the Jordan. Headed home that way," James moaned.

"I feel unclean just walking these paths," John replied to his brother, "and now we have to buy bread from these half-breeds."

"At least we get to view the rubble of their pagan temple," Judas interjected, his zealot heart a little too visible as he pointed out the ruins on the slopes of Mount Gerizim. "We showed them!"

"Enough!"

Andrew's retort brought the complaining to an abrupt end.

"Have we learned nothing from Jesus?" the young man continued. "Are our hearts any better than these Samaritans?"

Shocked eyes turned on the young fisherman, mouths open, ready to give him a history lesson he didn't need. But it was big brother Peter who got his reply in first, his raised hand stopping any others.

"Andrew is right. Have we not been listening to the Teacher?"

A few heads dropped in shame, recognising their racist hearts, while others sputtered, trying to justify their words.

"No," Peter continued. "Jesus said He had to go through Samaria... and I'm with Him. He also asked us to buy bread. So let's go before the market stalls close for the day."

"And remember," Andrew commented, wanting to have the last word, "our fathers Abraham and Jacob both bought land here..."

"And it's at Jacob's well that we've left Jesus... so let's get that bread and return to Him," his brother interjected. "Then we can all head home."

An uneasy silence cloaked the diverse group of disciples the rabbi from Nazareth had gathered around Him. They were twelve men with twelve differing opinions on most things, except for one. The Man they'd left at Jacob's well was no ordinary man. Of that they were sure. So the

87

agitated band temporarily tucked their prejudices out of sight as they trundled on to Sychar. Only the screech of the buzzard overhead invaded the uncomfortable stillness, its piercing call causing Andrew to look back suddenly in the direction of Jesus. The Master was out of sight by now, but the scraping of wood against his twisted back alerted him to a potential problem.

"Oh no!" Andrew shouted. "I didn't leave the bucket with Jesus!"

By the time the others turned in his direction the young man had whipped the folded bucket from his back stretching the leather and cross-sticks as if to prove his point.

"Andrew!"

There was no mistaking his brother's roar.

"I'll run back," Andrew responded, but Peter was in full flow, reminding him of his foolishness in leaving the Master with no means to draw water in this heat. The younger brother groaned, images of the circling buzzard not helping the situation. *How could I have been so stupid?*

"Enough!"

This time the voice belonged to Matthew.

"We didn't all need to come on this shopping trip. Some of us could have stayed behind with Jesus, but He didn't want us to. He was the one who sent us to the town."

All eyes were now on the former tax collector.

"For some reason the Master wanted to be alone. And, who knows, maybe a forgotten water bucket was part of the plan."

Andrew's shoulders relaxed at the touch of his sibling's calloused hands. Matthew's words made sense. And as he rolled the leather receptacle up again he couldn't help but wonder whether they would ever truly understand the Master's ways.

"Let's get the food, brothers," Peter said, "and we can head back to the well. I doubt Jesus is missing us too much."

Peter's laugh lightened the mood, softening their features to the surprise of the residents of Sychar.

What are all these Jews doing here?

"I'll be back soon. Look after your brother. Keep him in the shade."

"Where are you going, Mother?"

"Don't you see the sun in the sky, Little One? I'm heading to the well. The gossips should all have gone by now."

Aurora blew a kiss to her two children, stooping down to pluck a weed from the garden as she left. She balanced an extra-large jar on her hip, recognising that the tender plants needed water as much as her family did. The more she could cultivate for herself the less time she'd have to spend at the local market. As she stepped on to the path that bypassed the small town of Sychar, her free hand dropped to check the belt holding her folded bucket in place.

The woman looked weathered by more than the sun's rays, her hard life having added to the wrinkles on her olive skin. She took the path less trodden from her tiny home, set apart from the rest of the homes in Sychar. She was thankful that her current partner had taken her in when she had flashed her seductive eyes at him that day he stopped at the well on his way to Samaria. The well was a good place to meet men, especially at the time of day she made her daily visit. As she walked, she doubted this one would stay any longer than the rest of the men who had promised much but delivered no more than a bad reputation.

Men!

Since Aurora's birth, Mount Ebal had been true to its name. For the woman that no one in the village wanted to be seen with, it was indeed the 'Mount of Cursing'. Certainly others found it easy to point a finger at her. She was indeed a Law-breaker, but it wasn't something she did on her own… Swinging her braided hair in defiance, Aurora vented curses into the hot air against those who had been party to her sin. The culmination of husbands now dead, or having divorced her, had placed her on a plinth perfect for those determined to cast stones of judgment.

The piercing sound of a buzzard caused her to look heavenward. Groaning at the thought of some other poor creature about to be devoured by a predator from above, she set down her pot on the short grass.

Adonai, is there no end to this incessant shame? Must I live forever with my sin? Must I always choose the wrong? But how will I feed my children if there is no man in my life?

Her silent prayer, and the quiet tears of regret pooling in her dark eyes, were only ever evident on these hot trips to the well. She vowed never to display remorse in public for her immoral lifestyle. Arrogance and anger were the masks she hid behind when she met the stares and vitriol of others.

They might think I'm the only sinner in Sychar, but they'd know differently if they looked closer to home!

Rising to her feet, Aurora couldn't miss the majesty of Mount Gerizim opposite. The sight of the 'Mount of Blessing' pulled a distant memory from a place in her mind long since visited. In those moments, she heard her grandfather explain to her younger self how the priest had once stood with the Ark of the Covenant in the valley between the two mountains. Ebal, the old man had explained to his grandchildren, denoted the curse for breaking the Law of Moses while Gerizim promised blessing for those who kept it. But that blessing was only possible because of the presence of God represented by the Mercy Seat inside the Ark. God alone could forgive the sin of spoiled lives.

Blessing. Mercy. Forgiveness.

The words echoed in her head like sounds reverberating in Jacob's well. Yet, lifting her water jar again, she quickly dismissed the words of hope, this time giving voice to her thoughts: "That's not for the likes of me."

II

Jesus was glad of the rest, thankful for a short time free from questions, especially the kind that only sought dispute and entrapment rather than truth. His tired body winced against the scorching midday sun. Pulling the shawl over His head in an attempt at shade, the Master closed His eyes, resting weary bones on the well's hot stone lip. Even the noise of a buzzard overhead couldn't disturb those quiet short moments of solitude.

Solitude.

Jesus knew that the necessity for time away from the crowds, the disciples, the sick, the poor, the needy, not to mention the Pharisees, would be a constant battle in the days ahead. So much pain. So much need. So much sin. And so little time before...

How would that eager band of followers behave if they knew how little time they'd have with the rabbi from Nazareth? From beneath the shawl, He smiled at that thought, or was the smile for the near presence of the Father that enveloped Him there in the hills of Samaria? Or perhaps for the encounter that had necessitated His journey through this controversial territory? There was someone Jesus simply had to meet that day; and sitting under the noonday sun, He was only too aware that she was already on her way.

Aurora dragged her feet along the stony path. She couldn't quite put her finger on what was bothering her. She knew she should speed up having left the children alone yet again, but her pace was slow and her heart as heavy as the pot on her hip. The children were growing up far too fast, and she wasn't thinking merely in years. She sighed that her lifestyle had caused them pain so early in their lives; angry at the callous names thrown their direction by peers who didn't even know the meaning of the words they shouted. Sorry they had to endure scorn from adults who should have known better. After all, it wasn't their fault that their mother was a …

Why couldn't my father have waited? An all-too-frequent blame game raged in her head. *Why did he give me to his old friend for a wife? I was too young! He was too old! It was a servant he needed after his wife died… not a teenage bride!*

The memory of that day when the old shepherd came to her home, not simply to meet with his friend but to claim her as his bride, was forever seared on her brain. From as far back as she could remember, the man and his wife visited her family home when they needed to do business in Sychar. His wife usually brought some figs or honey as a gift for her cousin, Aurora's mother, and together they would make bread and catch up with family news while the men engaged in manly discussion on the roof. As she grew, Aurora loved to join the women. What better way to learn how to be a good homemaker than from this amazing duo? Grinding grain, making bread, and learning how to spice up a mutton stew was a rite of passage for every Samaritan girl. To be a good wife and mother was all that was expected of Aurora and her little sister. Early on she made that her aim. Surely if she was a good cook she would attract the interest of a good-looking boy from the town? So, she'd listen closely and follow their instruction carefully on all matters of wifely duties.

Often her mother's cousin would praise Aurora for her increasing skills, especially for her use of spice, something the men also complimented when they enjoyed a meal together. Aurora would blush and, recognising the changing of her body, she looked forward to the day she would hear similar appreciation from a husband of her own. There were eligible bachelors who'd cast an eye her way when she visited the market with her mother, or when she trudged along with the other young women towards the well. One day. She knew she still had much to learn but it didn't stop her teenage heart from dreaming.

Unfortunately, things began to change on the day her father's friend arrived without his wife. She was ill, he explained, anxiety written between the lines of his weather-beaten face. That day Aurora and her mother made food and baked bread before her mother set off to visit her cousin in the remote cottage an hour's walk from the town. The old couple had never been blessed with children, making it even more necessary for her to go. So Aurora was instructed to look after the children and keep house until her mother returned. A strange foreboding filled both heart and house as her mother's form disappeared beyond the horizon alongside her cousin's husband.

It was eight days before she returned. The day after her cousin's funeral.

A few months passed before the widowed shepherd visited again. That was not unusual in itself, considering his employment, but the family was shocked to see his unkempt appearance, and the way his flesh hung from his bones like a wrinkled blanket.

Aurora sighed, sorry for the man's loss and concerned that he would follow his wife before long… if the buzzards didn't get him first. The sight was not lost on her parents either – she could hear them talk late into the night, but not enough for her to make out exactly what was said. A few days later her father packed a few supplies and left home for a visit with his friend, leaving a very jittery wife behind. Aurora couldn't work out what the problem was, almost afraid to ask until it spilled out of her like the broth her mother had just slopped on to the floor.

"What is it, Mother? Are you ill?" she questioned, grabbing the pot handle from her mother's hands before she scalded herself.

Falling to her knees, hands covering her face, the older woman wept uncontrollably, unable to look her daughter in the eye. The girl wrapped her arms around her mother, who had not only given her life, but had lavished love on her every day since. She was warm, kind, gentle, and everything Aurora hoped she would be if the God of heaven granted her children of her own one day.

It seemed like forever before Aurora's mother shrugged off her eldest daughter's grip, while trying to compose herself enough to speak. Holding hands, faces now inches apart from each other, the older woman stuttered over her first few words.

"Y-y-your father and I think it's time you h-h-ad a h-h-husband."

The shock sent Aurora backwards, but this time it was her mother who held on to her.

"B-b-but who?" she replied, recognising that her mother's tears hardly indicated good news. "We haven't talked about it... I-I can't imagine who father has in mind."

"He's gone to arrange it today."

"But he's gone to see his friend. Is he stopping to speak with someone on his way home?"

"He's not stopping with anyone else Aurora."

"No, Mother! No!" The girl's shoulders were shaking by now. She wanted to run away – to escape the thoughts now threatening to drown her. "You can't mean it? Please tell me? Please tell me? It can't be father's friend! He's an old man!"

"Aurora." Her mother's voice had calmed in an attempt to take control. "Aurora, he's a kind man..."

"He's an old man, Mother!"

"I know child, but he needs a wife to look after him... you've seen how he's been since my cousin died... they had no children..."

No amount of reasoning could dampen the anger and fear in the teenager's heart. Her dreams were shattered as instantly as the pot she hurled across the room; her heart already tightly bound in chains no one could loose. No virile young man would ever take her in his arms and carry her to a marriage home built especially for her. There would be no happy band of singing maidens to accompany her with garlands of flowers and timbrels on her wedding day.

"I won't do it! I won't marry him!"

"You will, my love, you will. You have no choice."

You have no choice!

Four small words. Four words that Aurora allowed to mould her life from that moment on. Four words for which she could never forgive her father. Four words that broke her heart and started the dominoes of disaster falling in her life.

One month later, she left her father's home as the teenage bride of an old shepherd whose heart was buried with that of the only woman he could ever love. Aurora became his cook, housekeeper, and reluctant companion. The old man was cleaner and better fed but no happier, and in many ways he couldn't blame the young girl he'd watched growing up for her anger. He'd stolen her dreams, and now he got to watch her bitterness grow up close and personal.

As he lay on his deathbed, he wished her joy – but it wasn't to be.

According to the Law of Moses, she was now the property of his brother who'd conveniently turned up to claim the old man's belongings... including his young wife.

Leaving the old man's home that day, Aurora held her head high. She would neither show grief for the husband forced upon her, nor pleasure for the second husband who regarded her as little better than the rickety furniture he had also appropriated from his dead brother.

Now, all these years later, on her way to the well at noon, there was still no doubt in her mind who was to blame for her spoiled life... her father. She had never forgiven him, not even when he lay dying. Yet as she neared the well, a voice from deep within spoke so loudly to her that she almost dropped her water jar.

Aurora, you can't go on blaming others forever. One day you'll have to admit to your own wrongdoing.

III

Nearing the well, Aurora could see that she was going to have company after all.

The women of Sychar had long gone. In the early morning and just before dusk, this place would be full of noise – the kind she had grown to hate. Conversations that invariably started with, "Did you hear about... ?" Loose talk, innuendo, the giggling of teenagers, and the snapping of the impatient. There was a time when she couldn't wait for her daily dose of juicy news – the stuff that added a bit of excitement to the humdrum existence of home life. Unfortunately, it usually involved talk of the misfortunes of others, which could either be real, stretched, or even imagined. These days she was the main topic of conversation in all three genres. Gossip!

There'd be no such talk from this lone stranger at the well. A man. A Jew. A rabbi by the look of His shawl. No talk at all for that matter. It looked like she'd be bringing only water back from the well today. Stopping in her tracks, the spoiled woman of Samaria waited briefly for the place at the well to be vacated so she could get on with the task at hand. Even she was thirsty by this time.

Why doesn't He move away? What happened to the twenty feet rule? Come on, Jew, I'll never get my bucket filled with you sitting there. Is He asleep?

Aurora stamped her feet firmly as she took the final steps to the well, the jingling of her anklets confirming the approach of a woman. If He wasn't going to move then she'd get on with what she'd come to do. Her reputation couldn't be anymore tarnished than it already was. One step closer. No movement from the human statue. She might even get her water without Him waking up. Quietly slipping the bucket from her belt, Aurora made towards the edge of the well, unfolding the leather receptacle as she moved.

"Give me a drink."

Aurora jumped back, almost knocking over the water jar now propped up close to the well. The sleeping stranger was awake. His face now uncovered: His shawl draping strong, broad shoulders. Catching her breath the woman looked at the stranger. She was well used to sizing up the men that stopped here on their way to wherever. Missing the local women wasn't the only reason she visited Jacob's well at this time of the day. Journeys that started early in the morning were often halted at this main junction by noon for rest and refreshment. Occasionally, the travellers wanted more than water, and for a price she might even oblige. Some of those lucrative encounters had even started with a request like this. For Aurora it was time to test the waters.

His eyes caught hers.

What? He's looking me in the eye? What kind of a Jew is He? Mind you He does have nice eyes... and His hands are the hands of a man who's known hard work. Young. Maybe thirty or so?

Aurora stretched her lean body to its full height, straightening her veil, but not covering her face. She regained the distance she'd lost when the stranger startled her, coming to the edge of the well. He remained motionless.

Was He really just asking for a drink?

"How come you're asking *me* for a drink?"

She'd started and wasn't about to give into His request without finding out what He was up to.

"You're a Jew," she continued, her hand sweeping the air from His head to His feet as if to remind Him that His clothing gave Him away. "I'm a woman... and a Samaritan one at that..."

Still He looked at her, unflinching.

"... and you're asking the likes of me for a drink?"

The stranger's four-word request was the most confusing Aurora had ever heard. Everything this rabbi-of-sorts had been taught since He was a child was turned on its head by asking her for a drink. He knew full well the history between the Jews and the Samaritans. Bad blood didn't even cover it. He also knew the Law, probably even taught it. Yet this Man was breaking every law in the Book, especially those added by the Pharisees. Speaking to a woman was bad... speaking to a Samaritan was worse, but drinking from her bucket would defile Him!

Surely He can't be so thirsty that He'd render Himself unclean by asking her for a drink?

"If you knew the gift of God," the Man interrupted her mid-thought, "and who it is that is saying to you, 'Give me a drink,' you would have asked him, and he would have given you living water."

Gift of God? Living water? Has He got some magical drink?

This conversation was becoming more peculiar by the second, and she wondered if the sun might have affected the Man?

He doesn't even have a bucket!

Armed with that very thought Aurora pried further.

"Sir," she jumped right in. "You don't even have a bucket. This is a very deep well. How are you going to draw water, never mind this *living water* you speak of? Where does it come from?"

Pleased with her questioning, she continued with an enquiry that could set them on common ground, and perhaps encourage the Jew to make sense. Her heart was telling her that there was something about Him she liked. He was different from other men. And the thought of living water intrigued her.

"Are you greater than *our* father Jacob?" The woman wasn't quite sure whether she wanted to rub it in that the patriarch left the well to her people, or to remind the Man that they shared the same ancestry. "He not only gave us this well, but used it to quench the thirst of his family and his livestock."

The words had barely left her mouth when the Man sitting on the well replied, "Everyone who drinks of this water will be thirsty again, but whoever drinks of the water that I will give him will never be thirsty again."

A puzzled look crossed Aurora's face as He continued.

"The water that I will give him will become in him a spring of water welling up in eternal life."

Never to thirst again. Never to have to sneak to the well when others weren't around... or ever for that matter. What did she have to lose?

"Sir, give me this water," she responded, "so that I will not be thirsty or have to come here to draw water."

Imagine how that would change the burdens of life. People will start looking at me differently when I have something they don't.

But then the Man, whose name she did not yet know, threw a spanner in the works, just when she thought He could actually give her something that would change her life.

"Go, call your husband, and come here."

Aurora's heart sank. Why did it always come down to this? Could she not have the living water unless she had a husband? Was it all a trick? Was the stranger sitting on her well only interested in judging her, like all the other men in Sychar. Arrogance mixed with pain pushed her shoulders back and strengthened her legs.

"I have no husband," she answered, steeling herself for criticism.

"You are right in saying, 'I have no husband'... "

How could He know?

" ...for you have had five husbands, and the one you have now is not your husband."

Shocked, Aurora stood speechless. All the bravado she'd summoned now melted under the scorching sun, while the faces of the men she'd blamed for spoiling her life flashed through her mind. The husbands forced on her for expediency, money, and worst of all, as an excuse to maintain her decency. Saddest of all, the face of husband number five – the only one she'd grown to love – killed in a freak accident. His death had brought not only grief but also a determination that she'd do as she liked from then on – immoral, or not.

"What you have said is true."

Those final words of her life summary touched Aurora. They were laced with kindness, softening His knowledge of her sinful life by complimenting her confession.

Confession.

She hadn't really thought of her words as confession, but they were. And the look on His face spoke compassion, not judgment. Perhaps there was a way she could impress Him. Divert His thinking away from her, especially her sin. Something inside her wanted to please the Man who had happened to stop at her well today. A thought suddenly sprung to mind. Religion! Didn't religious men always like to talk religion?

"Sir," she said, starting with a compliment, "I recognise that you are a prophet."

He didn't immediately reject her words, so she foolishly attempted to engage a religious Jew in the very thing the Jews and the Samaritans had disagreed about for over five hundred years. Where should they worship? In Jerusalem, or on Mount Gerizim? The Man would not be drawn on that point but instead queried the Samaritans' very focus of worship.

"You worship what you do not know; we worship what we know, for salvation is from the Jews."

Aurora sensed that the stranger was changing the subject altogether, expressing that there was a day coming when geography and buildings – even temples – wouldn't determine the worship of God, adding that the divine presence of God would soon no longer need temples of stone to dwell in. She was mesmerised. Never before had she heard such a thing.

"But the hour is coming," the Man continued, "and is now here, when the true worshippers will worship the Father in spirit and truth, for the Father is seeking such people to worship Him."

Aurora's heart was racing. Her palms sweaty.

Could I learn to worship like that? Would the Father this Man was speaking about seek her to worship Him?

In those brief seconds as He spoke, the woman longed for her life to be changed. He hadn't condemned her. In fact, He had treated her better in those few minutes than any other man had in her whole life. According to the Law, she was ripe for stoning. But this Man spoke of salvation, true worship, and a Father who was seeking… perhaps even seeking her – a Samaritan, a woman – a woman spoiled by sin? How could that be?

Aurora sank on to the stony ground around the well, her leather bucket still firmly clasped in her hand. There was so much more she needed to know. Yet over her shoulder she could see a band of men heading towards the well.

"I know that Messiah is coming," she blurted out, eager to discover more before the others arrived. "You know who I mean, some call Him the Christ," she said looking into His eyes. "When He comes, He will explain everything to us."

And a smile spread across the stranger's face as He replied: "I who speak to you am He."

Aurora was dumbstruck. Her head was spinning. She couldn't respond. Wouldn't respond. Because deep in her heart she believed it was true. Dashing back along the road to Sychar she knew exactly what she had to do.

"Go," He had said.

And her feet couldn't carry her quick enough.

"Call your husband."

Watch out men of Sychar, I'm coming for you, like it or not.

"Come here."

I'll bring them back, Messiah, just wait and see!

And as she ran Aurora knew her life would never be the same again, for she was aware of something happening deep inside her. Could it be the *living water* the visitor to the well had spoken about?

IV

It was Peter who spotted it first.

Always out in front. Always wanting to please Jesus, the fisherman from Galilee stopped in his tracks as Jacob's well came into view. His sudden halt almost caused a pile-up of those following behind him on the road. Barely watching where they were walking, the men had been discussing Jesus' conversation with Nicodemus a short time before they'd set out from Jerusalem for their home in Galilee. This had been the first time they'd been apart from Jesus, and they'd used the opportunity to talk together about the strange idea of being born again that Jesus had challenged the religious leader with when he visited that night.

"Watch out Peter!" Andrew called, barely able to stifle a laugh at those who'd quite literally run into his brother.

Peter stood still and silent, gesturing in the direction of where they'd left Jesus. The twelve stood, shocked at the scene playing out before them.

Jesus was talking with a woman! A Samaritan woman! At a guess, an immoral woman!

Pace was added to their steps.

What did she think she was doing? What did she want from Jesus? How dare she? Why didn't Jesus move away from her? Surely He didn't actually want to speak with this woman?

Thoughts came thick and fast but none dared speak their concerns as they came closer to the well, making sure to keep their distance from the woman of course. They didn't want to be defiled by her. The air was thick with their disapproval. They only caught the last few words Jesus said to her: "I who speak to you am He," before she dashed past them, leaving her water pot behind.

Like a bunch of disapproving schoolboys they looked at Jesus, none of them brave enough to put their questions into words. Yet they realised He already knew what each was thinking. The Master could read them like a book. It seemed they could hide nothing from Him. So instead they broke the awkward silence by urging Him to eat. After all, maybe it was hunger that caused Him to act in such an unacceptable way.

But Jesus was having none of it.

"I have food to eat that you do not know about," He told them, hands raised in refusal of lunch.

Looking around, the men could see no sign of bread... the abandoned water jar, and crumpled bucket, the only evidence of anyone other than Jesus and the woman having been at the well recently. Those who muttered about the possibility that someone else had brought food to the rabbi, quickly realised that Jesus was speaking about a type of food they were only recently becoming aware of.

"My food is to do the will of Him who sent me," Jesus interjected, "and to accomplish His work."

The disciples were learning to hang on the rabbi's every word. They'd discovered that sitting at His feet was the best response to the many words and actions they didn't understand. So, not wishing to miss anything, the twelve dropped to the ground around Him. The bread could wait for now, they wanted to know about this 'food' Jesus was speaking about. He had a masterly way of using everyday things to explain the eternal. But as their minds rehearsed the rabbi's comments, He was already on to the fact that harvest was still four months away.

So then, how could He expect them to look around and see the fields ready to harvest?

Understanding that some farmers sow, while others reap made sense, but what was gathering fruit for eternal life all about?

Was Jesus expecting them to till the land now?

Sometimes it took a while for the penny to drop. But not always... perhaps helped on this occasion by the sound of a crowd approaching on the road from the town. Led by that woman, no less!

If thoughts had been audible, the noise from the disciples' minds would have clanged like clashing cymbals!

Fields white for harvest!

As the smile widened on Jesus' face, understanding began to register with those sitting around His feet. The 'food' the rabbi spoke about was nothing short of the satisfaction He received from doing "the will of Him who sent me". The twelve got to their feet waiting to see the Master wield the sickle.

Aurora couldn't believe what was happening.

She dared not look behind for fear it was all a dream. Yet the growing noise confirmed the truth. The townspeople believed her. They were following her to meet the Man at the well. Incredible! They were following *her*! The proud, the religious, the accusing, the arrogant, the gossips. Men. Women. Children. Even former husbands!

Barely minutes earlier, she had stormed through the gates of Sychar like a deranged woman, shouting for all she was worth for people to come and hear what she had to say. Initially men laughed, some even spat, while women wagged fingers, their faces contorted in criticism. But Aurora didn't care. For the first time in her life she *really* didn't care what they thought of her. The act was dropped. The mask no longer covering her sorrow for the life she lived, or the pain inflicted on her. She knew exactly who she was, and what she'd done, only this time she publicly confessed in order that others might meet the rabbi at the well.

It wasn't too long before a crowd gathered around the woman they normally crossed the square to avoid. She blurted it out. All about her journey to the well, and the Man she'd found there, sitting alone. Ignoring the crass innuendoes of meeting men at the well at noon, Aurora ploughed on, exasperated at times, but determined that she would tell them everything that had happened... everything that was said.

Soon, the crowd grew silent, and the woman couldn't help but wonder if the Man had done this? Did He make her speech eloquent so that she could deliver His message? Could He have something to do with the crowd listening when they normally didn't give her the time of day?

"I don't even know His name," she concluded, urging them to come back to the well with her, and see for themselves.

"Jesus," one of the stallholders called from the back of the crowd. "I heard the men with Him call Him 'Jesus' when they stopped to buy bread."

Jesus.

The very sound of His name caused Aurora's heart to beat faster.

"Then who will come with me to see Jesus for themselves?" she challenged. "I tell you this Man could be the Messiah!"

When she set off through the gate again, her son in her arms, and her daughter by the hand, Aurora couldn't bring herself to look behind her. But as she approached the well the look on the faces of Jesus' friends told her all she wanted to know.

She'd delivered Jesus' message and now the rest was up to Him.

V

What had just happened?

One thing was certain, Nathanael never dreamt they'd be heading back through Sychar's gates again today. Yet that's exactly what they were doing. Only this time, they were surrounded by Samaritans. The crowd was virtually carrying Jesus along, so much so that the disciples could barely get close to Him. Throwing a concerned glance in Philip's direction, the devout Jew was finding it difficult to have so many of these half-breeds, as he'd been taught to call them, rubbing up against him. Philip's facial expression stated what his mouth dared not utter, his arms still full of the bread they'd had no time to eat: that this was life on the road with Jesus.

Nathanael shrugged his shoulders, only too aware that the people his father had always told him to stay clear of were reacting with the same excitement he'd had on the day Jesus saw him sitting under the fig tree. Their scepticism had changed into curiosity, which was now morphing into amazement. Exactly the same route his own heart had taken on his first encounter with the Master. That thought quickly enabled the man Jesus had described back then as "an Israelite without deceit" to lower his prejudice, and allow it to be replaced by the pleasure of what he was witnessing. After all, he'd be a fool not to recognise what was happening here. It was nothing short of history in the making – Samaritans listening to a Jewish rabbi, Jews sharing bread with Samaritans – who would have thought it? Think what he'd have to tell his grandchildren.

This was revolution of a kind neither the Zealots nor the Romans could possibly have seen coming. Jesus was certainly stirring things up!

The disciples had never thought of the Samaritans as hospitable before. Probably because Samaria was only for passing through, not for stopping in. And the Samaritans were more than happy with that. Yet now sitting under shade offered first to their visitors, the twelve plus Jesus enjoyed more than the bread they'd purchased, along with water from the very jar filled on Aurora's second visit to the well.

What would the Jewish teachers think of them drinking from defiled vessels, given by Samaritan hands?

The thought dissipated as they observed how Jesus graciously accepted it. Following His lead, the disciples did the same, much to the pleasure of their new friends. And the sound of laughter was heard from both Jew and Samaritan.

"Sir?"

Silence fell on the group as the question hushed the merriment.

"Sir?" the woman repeated. "Can you tell us more about the 'living water' that You offered me at the well, please?"

And the woman held her children close, not wanting them to miss a word from the Man who was transforming her life. No longer spoiled. Now forgiven, and accepted… and thirsty for more of the living water.

Adapted from the story of the Woman of Samaria as recorded in John 4:4–43. The words of Jesus remain as recorded in the biblical text.

Spoiled: Life lessons

The struggle

Life is frequently unfair.

Let's face it. We have no control over the place of our birth, or even into which family we are born. Our sex and the colour of our skin is genetically coded *in utero*. The very cultural rules we will be expected to abide by are already set before we arrive on the scene. The United Nations Declaration of Human Rights, adopted in 1948, declares the basic rights of every human being to include life, liberty, and security – but the reality often strays far from the thirty printed articles that promise so much.[3]

There are few here, in what is termed the 'first world', who would say their lives have exactly run to plan or are the culmination of their dreams. Many see where they are now more as a product of circumstances over which they had, or still have, very little control. A rationale that often results in discontent, and unhappiness.

More than one thousand years had passed between the life of Abigail and that of the Woman of Samaria. Yet little had changed for women during that time.

To understand the woman in this story better, we need to be aware of the culture behind her status as a woman, and as a Samaritan. In the recounting of the incident, the Apostle John decided that the woman's name was not as important as the historical and spiritual fallout of what took place over those few days. His focus was on what Jesus did, rather than on identifying the woman. Yet, even without a name, Jesus treated this woman as an individual of worth.

In my retelling I chose to name this nameless woman, to help us identify with her as a real person. I once heard it said that to be nameless is akin to being invisible. So, I called her Aurora, after the Roman goddess, in light of the Roman influence in the area that housed the temple to Caesar Augustus, a mere six miles from Sychar. The Samaritans' mixed-race history dated back to the Assyrian conquest of the Northern Kingdom in 721 BC, and their subsequent intermarriage with Gentiles.

But it didn't stop there. The Greeks complicated things further by using Samaria as their base when they controlled Jewish territory in 303 BC, further diluting the gene pool. Then Herod the Great added to the confused identity by building the Roman temple in 19 BC, encouraging large numbers of Romans to visit the area and mix with the locals.

Samaria was indeed a culturally diverse place. In spite of this, the Samaritan's religious affiliation had remained unchanged. They held to the Torah of Moses, and the worship of God on Mount Gerizim. This inevitably led to fierce differences with the Jews, who not only believed in racial purity but in a religion that included the Law *and* the Prophets. For them, the only place for worship was the Temple in Jerusalem that housed the Ark of the Covenant. Tension between the two races remained profound – and, at times, violent. The most orthodox of Jews even chose to cross the Jordan and take the longer route between the north and south of the country rather than set foot on Samaritan soil.

This was the culture in which the Woman of Samaria was raised. A confusing hotchpotch of identity, in a community despised by its nearest neighbours. Yet it was also a community that had no mercy when it came to how it treated its own if they thought they'd crossed the morality line – a situation not exclusive to Samaria, and one in which most of the blame was attributed to women. Remarkably, a woman was always seen as the guilty party, even when it came to immoral practices that involved both sexes!

To be a woman in this era was far from easy.

Education was exclusively for your brothers, while outdoor activities were only to facilitate household chores – shopping, gathering wood, and fetching water from the well. Girls were taught to be good wives to the husbands arranged for them by their fathers, or by other males in the family if your father was dead. Apart from keeping house, and caring for the children, men decided on all other matters. Although, in fairness, very few life choices were available to anyone. Life was all about survival, which necessitated hard work for little reward, hopefully resulting in putting food on the family table and paying your taxes. In the majority of cases, an arranged marriage was not an act of unkindness. It's not that eastern fathers did not love their daughters, but a married daughter was one less mouth to feed for a man who was already struggling to making ends meet for his family.

I wish I could say it was different today, but for many that is not the case. Millions continue to live a hand-to-mouth existence. In some cultures women continue to be seen as subservient – mere possessions to use as men see fit; innumerable lives spoiled by the unfortunate place of their birth and the injustice of others. Sadly, we have little cause for smugness, as the abuse of women scarring our own nation is little better than the cultural behaviour we frown on from a distance. We have much still to learn.

By the time this particular woman met Jesus at Jacob's well, her life was well and truly spoiled. Spoiled by the culture surrounding her; spoiled by the choices made on her behalf, spoiled by the unfairness of life, and by the unkindness of others. Yet, until this divine encounter, she seemed unwilling to acknowledge the part she herself played in her spoiled life – her personal sin.

Thankfully, Jesus is in the business of transforming lives, and challenging cultures too. However, change takes place one person at a time, and one changed life can impact a whole community. Look at what happened in Sychar!

Justice

Justice has become a buzzword in our twenty-first-century world. However, its practical outworking varies in the extreme. One person's justice has the potential for creating another's injustice.

Inequalities of all kinds have always been with us. And the concepts of fairness, integrity, and honesty are battles that every generation continues to fight.

The word 'justice', or what has become known as 'natural justice', is commonly used in respect of punishment, or revenge, particularly concerning a wrongdoer. When the criminal is finally caught and punished, it will often illicit a response of 'they got what they deserved'. There is something in our DNA that wants us to see the right thing done. Yet, at the same time, we find it difficult to conceive that is exactly what God requires... justice.

In Scripture, justice and righteousness are entwined. God is a holy God (Isaiah 6:3). We are sinful people (Romans 3:23). Sin is contrary to His nature, and so justice demands punishment (Romans 6:23). But God is also merciful and loving. Therefore, in order that His justice – the right thing – is done, Christ took the judgment for our sin on Himself when He died on the cross. Justice was satisfied (2 Corinthians 5:21), and we can be forgiven by walking the bridge of repentance into a relationship with this holy God (1 John 1:9).

Justice – doing the right thing – was God's idea, and since we are created in His image (Genesis 1:27), it follows that it should also be close to our heart. That was certainly true of Jesus.

We may think that 'Mission Statements' are a relatively new development, often publicly displayed on the walls of hotels, businesses, government facilities, and more. But we are wrong. It was Jesus who first publicly declared His Mission Statement when He read from the prophet Isaiah (61:1–2) on a visit to the synagogue in Nazareth (see Luke 4:18). And it was all about justice.

> "The Spirit of the Lord is upon me,
> because he has anointed me
> to proclaim good news to the poor.
> He has sent me to proclaim liberty to the captives
> and recovering of sight to the blind,
> to set at liberty those who are oppressed,
> to proclaim the year of the Lord's favour."
> **(Luke 4:18–19)**

Jesus was not a political figure, but He was deeply concerned about justice for the marginalised, mistreated, and poor.

First on the Saviour's Mission Statement was a declaration that He was anointed by God's Spirit to "proclaim good news to the poor". Poor spiritually? Poor monetarily? Yes, and yes. Jesus demonstrated to us the need to reach everyone with the gospel, whatever his or her social class. God has no favourites (Romans 2:11). Just as sin is universal, so is God's mercy. Jesus preached both as a priority.

There is no doubt that this prophetic declaration, fulfilled by Jesus, can be understood from a purely spiritual stance. The poor, captive, blind, and oppressed all fit the picture of those living in spiritual darkness. However, while Jesus' mandate was salvation for a lost world (Luke 19:10), the practical outworking of this prophesy in Isaiah 61 included meeting the needs of the whole person – as was evident in Jesus' encounter with the Woman of Samaria.

Jesus broke all the misplaced cultural rules of gender and race when He spoke to the woman He met at Jacob's well that day. His conversation was not merely one of necessity – He was thirsty after all – but, rather, He chose to engage with her at length on matters normally only discussed by men with other men. This alone elevated her position in a world where equality was a misnomer.

Only after affirming her value as a woman did Jesus then address her social circumstances. It was obvious that her own community had rejected her. Why else would she visit the well at a time when she could be guaranteed no one else from her village would be there? Yet Jesus did not condemn the woman, in spite of being aware of her immorality.

"The one you have now is not your husband," was Jesus' reply after asking her to go and call her husband.

Her immorality was not in having had five husbands. Jesus understood only too well the burden of womanhood in His day. The woman's sin was in her current immoral lifestyle. Yet He did not come to condemn the one who was already condemned by all and sundry (John 3:17). Instead He came to offer her "living water" (John 4:10). Later, John explains that the "living water" Jesus spoke about was "the Spirit, whom those who believed in Him were to receive" (John 7:37–39).

Throughout Scripture the Holy Spirit is alluded to by water. He is the "living water" that cleanses and gives life. It is His life within us that guarantees our eternal inheritance (Ephesians 1:13–14): His life not only blesses us but flows through us to bless the lives of others.

Jesus didn't only offer the Woman of Samaria a life forgiven, cleansed by the Spirit living in her, He also brought her dignity and acceptance. The Saviour showed us that natural justice could not be separated from social justice. According to Jesus, both come in the same package. The good news of salvation that we preach should be laced with the same human compassion that Jesus demonstrated to the Woman of Samaria (John 4:4–42), the hungry (Matthew 14:13–21), the sick (Luke 5:12–15), the grieving (John 11:33–36), and the oppressed (Mark 5:1–20).

God makes it clear in Micah 6:8 what He requires of us: "to do justice, and to love kindness, and to walk humbly with your God".

Just like Jesus.

The blame game

We live in a society where when something goes wrong it's always someone else's fault.

Undoubtedly many do suffer because of the actions of others. It's foolish to think otherwise, but there does seem to be a universal desire to find someone else to blame for all of life's ills. Too often we operate on the premise that it's never my fault therefore someone else must be held to account.

There's a humorous sketch in the musical *West Side Story* where a street gang are rehearsing the reasons for their misdemeanours to the local beat-cop Officer Krupke. It has the audience rolling in the aisles as the reprobates try to explain away their law breaking by blaming everyone else for their unacceptable behaviour. With doleful eyes and the cupping of their handsome faces, they move quickly with their excuses, laying the blame at the feet of all and sundry. No one escapes. Mother, father, grandparents, brother, sister – even the social worker, psychiatrist, and judge – each one is blamed as the cause of their reprobate life. It's not their fault, they plead on bended knee, with hands beating against their hearts… they are just misunderstood.

It's hilarious! Why? All good comedy mimics life, and in this sketch we view life as it is. We see ourselves in it. We hear all the excuses laid bare. Excuses that we've perhaps made for ourselves, and others. If only I'd been born into a different family, or another neighbourhood, or gone to the school across town, or got that job, or married someone else? My life would have been so different… And from that we extrapolate that it can't really be my fault that I find myself in this situation.

Owning up is no fun. And real life isn't funny.

There is no clear evidence in the biblical text that the Woman of Samaria engaged in the blame game in respect of her life circumstances. However, those few words of Jesus in John 4:18, "for you have had five husbands," speak volumes concerning her social status. This woman would have had no say in any of her five marriages. Therefore, I have chosen to give voice to the probability of her response to her life experience, especially as by this time she had made the personal choice of a sinful liaison in place of another arranged marriage.

Unfortunately, two wrongs don't make a right, as the old proverb says.

This sad woman isolated herself further from her community by her actions, but not from the understanding and mercy of a compassionate Saviour (John 4:17–18).

Many of life's difficulties are not our fault, but if we are ever to move on and experience release from the grip of damage inflicted on us then we need to:

- **Revisit the wrong**, asking God to give us a clear picture of what actually happened. Hurt has a way of fertilising our memory of things, even exaggerating the damage inflicted. What did that person, community, *actually* say or do? Was it all their fault? Could I have done anything differently?

- **Adjust our response** to the wrong committed against us. If someone within the church fellowship, or another fellow Christian, has wronged you in some way, then the Bible has very clear instructions set out in Matthew 18:15–18 as to how this should be dealt with.

  Speak to the person and attempt a resolution without involving anyone else (verse 15).

  If that is unsuccessful then take two or three witnesses with you as evidence to the concerns of both parties (verse 16). Different voices may encourage reason and restoration.

  If the offending party will still not repent, then – and only then – should the matter be brought before the church for guidance and discipline (verse 17).

  Remember that the point in facing another person with their wrongdoing is not to exact judgment but rather to lead to the restoration and healing of both parties. Much harm has been done to individuals, churches, and the very name of Christ by not following the principles listed in this passage. Instead, gossip, backbiting, and additional hurt result, even culminating in relationships, families, churches, and communities being torn apart. However, it is unfortunate that certain individuals will never admit their sinful behaviour. So rather than allow their actions to cause bitterness to further damage your life it is time to…

- **Surrender our expectations** of change – in either the person or the situation – to God. If not, bitterness, anger, and even revenge become the sins we will have to deal with. There comes a time when we must give it up, even if it means forgiving the perpetrator in spite of their refusal to seek our forgiveness. (See the notes on forgiveness in the section 'Failure: Life lessons'.)

Only God can give the kind of grace required for this godly response, and only God can return peace to a heart filled with pain.

Tough stuff. But then we have not been promised a trouble-free life. Jesus said in John 16:33, "In the world you will have tribulation. But take heart; I have overcome the world."

Pain is part of life's package, but you are not alone in either situation or experience, for Jesus has promised His presence with you right where it hurts (Isaiah 43:2).

However, there are times when the blame rightly lands firmly at our feet. What should we do then?

Confession

When Jesus first confronted the Woman of Samaria about her sin (John 4:16–18), she responded honestly, and then quickly sidestepped the issue by trying to change the subject. Regrettably, she chose to head down the 'religious' path to escape further investigation of her sinful life. Jesus played along only briefly before bringing her back to her heart's greatest need – salvation.

"The woman said to him, 'I know that Messiah is coming (he who is called Christ). When he comes, he will tell us all things'" (John 4:25).

"Jesus said to her, 'I who speak to you am he'" (John 4:26).

Making excuses, blaming others, or hiding behind religion holds us back from dealing with the main problem – our sin. Only confession (admission of our wrongdoing and rebellion against God) and repentance (sorrow and a turning away from sin) can lead to God's forgiveness. Forgiveness is not gained by packing our lives with as much religion as possible, but based only on trusting what Christ accomplished on the cross at Calvary.

"For Christ also suffered once for sins, the righteous for the unrighteous, that he might bring us to God" (1 Peter 3:18).

Remarkably, forgiveness delivers more than the cleansing of our sin. It restores the relationship God intended for us to have with Him while giving peace to our hearts. Augustine of Hippo, early church father and

Bishop of Hippo AD 396–430, explained that fact perfectly when he said: "Thou has made us for thyself, O Lord, and our heart is restless until it finds its rest in thee."[4]

Confession and repentance lead to God's forgiveness through Christ, which results not in a change in circumstances per se but radical transformation in us.

"If we confess our sin," we are told in 1 John 1:9, "he is faithful and just to forgive us our sins and to cleanse us from all unrighteousness."

Jesus: compassionate Saviour

Having spent so much time in this remarkable story I can see why John left the woman without a name. Perhaps when the apostle first met her, he thought very much the same as other Jewish men did about women in general, and Samaritans in particular. I imagine by the time the group of travellers left Samaria two days later John's prejudice had changed, or at least was undergoing change.

To John this incident was all about Jesus.

This particular gospel writer wanted his readers to focus on what the Saviour thought, said, and did when He came in contact with someone most people would have crossed a river to avoid. The Woman of Samaria did have a name, she did live with rejection and pain, and she was just like us – she was a sinner. Perhaps naming her might have been a distraction, but ignoring her encounter with Jesus was not an option.

Just as we might say of a growing boy, "he's his father's son", indicating such likeness in more than looks, so it was with Jesus. He was indeed His Father's son. The Father never gave up with the people He called "His treasured possession" (Deuteronomy 7:6), in spite of their persistent stubbornness and rebellion (Deuteronomy 9:6–7). His special love for them was not because of any attributes they had, since God frequently had to deal with their wayward nature, but because it was from the Jewish nation that the Saviour would come.

Jesus was a Jew.

Yet remarkably God sent His Son to redeem, not only the Jews, but also the whole world (John 3:16).

After one of the disciples – Philip – asked Jesus to show them the Father, Jesus simply told him, "Whoever has seen me has seen the Father"

(John 14:9). Something Philip had obviously not fully understood, though Jesus had earlier declared to questioning Jews in the Temple, "I and the Father are one" (John 10:30).

Jesus was indeed His Father's Son in every way. We read in John 4:4, "He had to pass through Samaria", when in fact He could have taken another route. The Father always had cared for His special people, even those as errant as the Samaritans. Therefore, it's unlikely that Jesus would have missed the opportunity to give them the gospel, making it essential for Him to go through Samaria. There was more on His mind than meeting with a certain sad and sinful woman when He chose His itinerary that day. However, the bigger picture being played out in this story doesn't change the fact that she was on His mind – this woman mattered to Jesus.

Throughout the Gospels, we witness Jesus' concern for individuals, those whose lives have been spoiled by injustice, cruelty, disease, poverty, and sin. And John's record of Jesus' meeting with the Woman of Samaria provides us with a window to the compassionate heart of a Saviour who doesn't give up on us... whatever our circumstances, however serious our sin.

- **Jesus seeks us out:** "For the Son of Man came to seek and save the lost," the Saviour explained after He called the reprobate Zacchaeus down from his hiding place in the tree (Luke 19:1–10). In fact, right from the Garden of Eden, when Adam and Eve tried to hide following their disobedience (Genesis 3:9), God has been seeking out the sinner.
- **Jesus places value on our lives,** stating that the two-for-a-penny sparrow can't fall to the ground without the Father knowing about it, therefore we are certainly of even greater value (Matthew 10:29–31). God sees us, knows us, and cares about the disasters of our lives, even when no one else does. We are not invisible to the Master. He is El Roi, "the God who sees me" (Genesis 16:13 NLT).
- **Jesus put the needs of others above His own reputation**: In Samaria, He spoke with a woman, a cultural taboo that shocked even his disciples (John 4:27). In Nain, Jesus touched an open coffin (Luke 7:11–17) rendering Himself ceremonially unclean for seven days (Numbers 19:11). In Galilee, He put His hands on a man with leprosy and healed him (Mark 1:40–45), declaring no one as untouchable. We frequently read of Jesus being moved with compassion for those in need. (See

Mark 8:2-3; Matthew 9:36; Matthew 20:34). Jesus wasn't afraid of what others said about Him, He did what He knew was right.

- **Jesus ministered spiritual truth to everyone,** including the woman He met at Jacob's well. The gospel message of sin, repentance, forgiveness and new life through belief in Jesus, and the indwelling Holy Spirit (John 4:13-14), was made available to everyone, not only to the self-proclaimed religious.
- **Jesus involves us in spreading the Good News:** In John 4:16, "Jesus said to her [the Samaritan woman], 'Go, call your husband, and come here.'" By the time their conversation had ended she dashed back to Sychar and told the whole town about Jesus… and they not only listened to her but also followed her back to meet Him (John 4:28-30). Jesus does not require us to be preachers, or missionaries, but rather to be willing to share what we know about Him, and what He's done in our lives. Sharing the gospel is not a job; it's a lifestyle. After the resurrection, and before Jesus' ascension, the Saviour gave His final command to His followers. A command just as relevant to us today: "Go therefore and make disciples of all nations, baptizing them in the name of the Father and of the Son and of the Holy Spirit" (Matthew 28:19).

The gospel message is transformational in lives spoiled by sin, or devastated by the circumstances of life.

When Jesus left Samaria a few days later, the Woman of Samaria was still a woman, still a Samaritan, still a widow, and still living in poverty, and possibly rejection. It might seem as if nothing had changed – but, in fact, so much had. She had experienced compassion, understanding, and the knowledge of how her life could be changed from the inside. Jesus' subsequent teaching to the townsfolk (John 4:39-43) hopefully began to challenge their attitudes and treatment of others, but the externals of the Woman of Samaria's spoiled life were already under reconstruction, thanks to Jesus.

"Therefore, if anyone is in Christ, he is a new creation. The old has passed away; behold, the new has come."
2 Corinthians 5:17

Spoiled: Taking a closer look

For personal or group study

Study questions

1 Read John 4:4–12. Immerse yourself in the story. Has your opinion of this woman changed since reading the retelling? What has changed, and why?
2 Gossip – the sharing of information negatively, using distorted truth – is destructive. How should we behave when unchecked information is passed on to us? See Proverbs 11:12 and 1 Timothy 5:13.
3 Spend time meditating on Micah 6:8. How do you rate yourself on what the Lord requires of you?
4 Is social justice a gesture or a lifestyle? Does it matter? Back up your response with Scripture.
5 Jesus often used the 'everyday' to explain the eternal. In this account, He used 'living water' to communicate the Holy Spirit living within the believer to the Woman of Samaria (John 4:10). In what other ways does Jesus describe Himself through ordinary elements?
6 Compare John 3:17 with Romans 6:23. How can they sit side by side?
7 In his letter to the Roman believers, the Apostle Paul states clearly, "I am not ashamed of the gospel, for it is the power of God for salvation to everyone who believes" (Romans 1:16). The woman at the well didn't hesitate to tell others about Jesus… what about you?
8 What mission statement would best describe your life? Does it need any adjustment?

4

GUILT
JUDAH

GUILT
JUDAH

I

c. 1704 BC

"She's done WHAT?"

Judah sprang to his feet, eyes flashing like lightning. The courier stepped back; fearful the master might strike him with the clenched fist now swiping the air. The young man had never seen Judah this angry before; the space between them thick with expletives. A crowd quickly gathered. Friends and servants desperate to know what could possibly have set off such fury in this son of Jacob.

"Who told you this nonsense?" Judah asked, his face barely inches from that of the terrified messenger.

"It... it... it is common knowledge, Sir," the young man stuttered.

The assembling crowd mumbled and muttered, questioning shoulders rising and falling in the melee.

"Your friend told me to tell you that Tamar, your daughter-in-law, has behaved immorally..."

"Disgraceful!" shouted one.

"Harlot!" yelled someone else.

"Stone her!" roared another. Each catcall interrupting the young man's message.

"And," he attempted to finish: "she's pregnant!" His closing words provoked hissing and jeering from the crowd.

"Tamar?" questioned one of the bystanders. "Wasn't she wife to two of your sons, Judah... before they died... in suspicious circumstances?"

The angry men stilled at the question, waiting for Judah's reply. Tamar. Yes. She was the one. The one Judah blamed for the death of his two eldest sons. Rumour at the time blamed God's judgment for Er's death. He had always been up to no good. Something Judah knew but didn't want to believe. Yet to die suddenly, and so young? It was a mystery. But Onan? Everyone knew he didn't want to take his brother's wife on just to give her a son. A son that would always be seen as his brother's son. A son that would divide the inheritance, leaving less for his own family. No, Onan made sure Tamar wouldn't become pregnant by him.

"Tamar?" asked another. "No one's seen her for years."

The men gossiped like a group of chittering women around the town's

119

well, leaving Judah fuming at the humiliation Tamar had brought to his tent.

"Didn't you send her back to her father's home, Judah… after Onan died?"

"None of this matters!" Judah screamed, his anger unabated. "She will pay for her sin, and the shame she has brought to this house, and to my sons."

Turning to the young messenger, who by this time had dried the sweat from his brow, Judah pronounced judgment on the absent daughter-in-law.

"Bring her out!" he told the men around him. "Bring her out," vitriol spewing from his mouth. "She'll burn to death for this!"

Quickly a band of Judah's comrades and servants were sent off towards Tamar's village to exact judgment. Judah, however, stayed at home stewing in self-righteous indignation. He was a coward, happy to send others to do his dirty work. Yet, as the sounds of the horses disappeared into the distance, a promise made to this young woman nagged at Judah's heart. Hadn't he promised Tamar that one day she would have his youngest son in marriage. Judah was well practised at arguing with his heart. After all, Tamar wasn't the first to prick his conscience.

"This is different," Judah tried to reason with himself. "This is different," he repeated, his head now cupped in his hands. "Tamar will pay. She'll pay for her sin!"

As the hours passed, the wine did nothing to pacify the agitation in Judah's heart. On the horizon he could see the dust of an approaching rider. *Good,* he thought, *the deed must be done.* Rising to his feet, Judah nervously awaited the horse and rider's arrival. *It must be one of Hirah's men sent ahead with news,* he thought.

The rider jumped to the ground, reaching for a small leather pouch as he did so. Judah squeezed his eyes together against the lowering sun. *Is that my staff he is pulling from across his back? Surely not?*

Judah could feel his legs weaken beneath him as the man quietly walked the short distance towards the entrance of Judah's tent. The man's eyes met his with a look of disdain that even his wine-induced stupor couldn't miss. Arrogance briefly stiffened Judah's resolve.

"Is it done?"

"Master, the woman you sent us to kill asked that you see these items before the judgment is sanctioned."

Judah's head spun as the messenger pulled a cord from inside the pouch. The cord was strung through a small clay cylinder with a signet on the end. By now, Judah's heart was pounding in his chest with the same fervour as his desire to run away. So loud was its beating that he barely heard what was said next.

"Sir, Tamar asks that you identify to whom these things belong," he said, planting the staff upright into the ground as he did so. "She says that the man who owns them is the father of her child."

The temple prostitute at Enaim! It was Tamar!

The horizon no longer held still; it swayed behind the man who had now become Judah's accuser. The tables had turned. Judah was in the dock and found wanting. No, it was more than that – he was found guilty. Guilty of reneging on the promise of giving his youngest son to Tamar in marriage. Guilty of blaming this woman for the deaths of his sinful sons. Guilty of seeking a Canaanite prostitute at a pagan festival. Guilty of the hypocrisy of passing judgment on Tamar when his own heart burned with the shame of the past and the culpability of the present. And still the man stood, towering over Judah like some other-worldly being, waiting for his response.

All Judah could do was whisper, for his strength was waning. His body felt as weak as his will had done that day on the road to Timnah, when he saw the veiled woman he thought was a prostitute. Now he needed to dismount his arrogance, and for once in his life own up to his wrongdoing.

"These items belong to me," his voice rasped.

Judah stiffened at the sound of the gasps from the crowd now gathered around the messenger. The self-righteous Hebrew was more Canaanite than he would ever choose to admit. Seems that you become like the people you live with after all.

"It appears that the woman… Tamar… is more righteous than I am," he continued. "I wronged her when I did not keep my promise to give her my son Shelah as a husband."

With all eyes now firmly fixed on Judah, he offered his final response to the rider waiting to return to the condemned woman.

"Let her go free. I am the guilty one."

As disgrace now filled the air, the messenger mounted his horse and galloped out of sight. Then Judah, son of Jacob and grandson of Isaac, retreated into his tent knowing full well that Tamar wasn't the only one he had wronged. And he wept.

II

"Elohim, God of my fathers? How did I ever get to this place where guilt dogs my steps, condemning me at every turn on life's road?"

It had been hours since Judah had risen from lying with his face on the floor of his tent. Hours since those he'd sent to kill Tamar had returned. Darkness had fallen, yet still he heard voices outside his door; debate about whether they should interrupt him rumbled on. Some were angry. Others embarrassed by what they had heard, but each one anxious to speak with Judah, whether friend or servant. But Judah was having none of it. While the flap of his tent remained fastened, no one could enter. Only Hirah, the Adullamite, dared to address Judah directly through the leather walls.

"Judah, my friend," he called, silencing all other voices. "Judah, may I enter? We are concerned for you. Let me bring you some bread and wine?"

"Go home, Hirah. Leave me alone with my God. It has been too long since He and I have spoken."

"Judah?"

"Go home, Hirah."

From his position on the floor Judah could hear his dear friend Hirah send the other men home to bed. As their torches moved further away, the darkness of the night collided with the darkness of Judah's soul.

Hirah it was whose friendship and love of fun had enticed Judah to leave his father's camp for the excitement of Canaanite life in Chezib. The Hebrew had grown tired of family at every turn; tired of the rules of Hebrew life; tired of the constant reminder of Yahweh's hold over them. Worshipping the many pagan gods was much more thrilling than worshipping the One of whom his grandfather Isaac and father Jacob continually reminded him and his eleven brothers of.

Ten – not eleven...

The torturous reminder erupted suddenly from a place Judah preferred to forget. He'd spent years burying that memory... or trying to. Hirah wasn't the only reason he'd left home. It was the never-ending grief of his old father; the secret glances of nine brothers who'd each promised they would never again speak about what happened at Dothan; the innocent face of Benjamin that greeted him each day with the same exuberance of his older brother.

Joseph.

It was Joseph who invaded Judah's dreams and tormented his soul. Hirah may have tempted Jacob's fourth son, but Judah now realised it was Joseph's memory that had sent him seeking peace away from home. Joseph. Forever gone, yet always present.

Joseph. I'm sorry.

Shame kept Judah's head bowed, while a Presence in the room led him back – back to the place where he'd lost his soul – back to the only place he'd find it again.

20 years earlier

"This well is dry," Levi shouted to his brothers. "We'll need to find another one."

"How can the pasture be good here at Dothan, and the well is dry?" Judah asked Reuben, keen to learn the ways of the wilderness.

"Something must be blocking it," Reuben replied, all the while scanning the fields around. "Issachar, go check that other well," he ordered, pointing in the direction of a low round wall partially obscured by scrubby grass.

Judah loved the way his eldest brother took charge. Even out here, there were always squabbles between the ten brothers. Sibling rivalry was rife – all the more so where four mothers were involved. Gaining recognition in such a complicated family was tough when your place was further down the line – unless your name was Joseph... But out here with the sheep, Reuben was boss. Judah liked that. Fancy coats were no good to a shepherd. You can't shear a sheep when your sleeves reach your wrists. Whatever Jacob said about Joseph – or more accurately, whatever Joseph said about himself – sheep were the family business. Sheep made them wealthy. Dreamer-boy was soft. He'd never make a shepherd. His head was too full of puffed-up imaginings of self-importance. Judah was convinced that Jacob would come to his senses soon enough, or at least that's what he said as ten brothers led scores of sheep in search of good pasture.

Heat and dust were constant annoying companions as both flock and shepherds made their way to the slightly cooler north. Shepherding was not an easy life but returning with a full flock, fattened by good grazing, would surely put the brothers in their father's good books. Lately, Joseph was commanding even more attention from Jacob than usual. It seemed the older Rachel's firstborn became, the more their father fussed over him. He might as well have 'Favourite' branded on his forehead!

Judah tossed, struggling to sleep in the cold, the heat having disappeared as rapidly as the sun had made its departure. Now as he lay gazing into the vastness of the starry canopy overhead, Jacob's fourth son couldn't help but remember the dream that had outraged even their father. The ensuing rebuke made Judah smile on this night far away from home.

"Joseph!" Jacob had exclaimed in full hearing of the whole family. "What is it with these dreams? Where is your respect? Sun, moon, and eleven stars bow down to you, Joseph? Do you honestly believe that your mother and I, along with your brothers, will do you obeisance? Nonsense!"

Pity you didn't put him in his place more often, Father.

Recounting the reprimand caused Judah to chuckle as the stars above him twinkled like the gems he hoped to own one day. He was also furious with Joseph's grandiose ideas. After all, Joseph was the eleventh son in a society that believed in the privilege of the firstborn. In their family, that was Reuben – Judah's oldest brother to Jacob's first wife. Surely that counted for something.

But did it?

Growing up, Judah had heard the story of how his father Jacob had cheated his older brother Esau out of his birthright. *Something about a hard day's hunting and a bowl of lentil stew,* Judah thought, as his eyelids grew heavy. *It won't happen again, Joseph. Just you wait. Reuben will not be robbed like Esau. I'll make sure of that.*

"J-u-d-a-h!"

Hearing his name as if called from some faraway place Judah reluctantly pulled himself from the deep sleep to which he had finally succumbed.

"What?" he yelled, pulling his shoulder away from Zebulun's rough shaking.

"Judah! Wake up!" the boy shouted. "Wolves! Reuben said to come quickly!"

The youngest of the shepherds looked terrified as Judah suddenly jumped to his feet, igniting a torch in the fire as he followed the speedy

Zebulun. The sheep were scattering everywhere. Judah could hear the growling and snapping of the vicious beasts as he neared the edge of the flock where his brothers held the line between them and the sheep. He and the frightened Zebulun lengthened the line of defence, shocked that the pack hadn't run away by now.

Reuben bellowed orders to his men with military precision, ordering some to aim their slingshots at the beasts' heads, while the remainder continued to wave flaming torches at the attackers. Yelping started to fill the air.

"Aim for the one in the middle," Judah interjected. "She looks like the leader of the pack!"

A cascade of sharp stones rained down just where Judah said, and with a howl the injured beast stumbled, finally turning and running back into the night. As the others followed their leader, the men cheered, waving torches and slings in their hands. This time they'd won. But Judah had no doubt the pack would return. They'd need to move the flock on tomorrow.

It was only when the wolves fled that Judah was able to see the destruction left in their wake. Three lambs lay dead, bodies torn apart. Nearby, two ewes panted their final breaths as blood pooled beneath their heads from bite marks left in their necks. Zebulun's shocked expression drew sympathy from Judah. He remembered only too well the first time he had seen a dying sheep. With a sympathetic hand on the boy's shoulder, he said: "Com'on, Zeb, time to round up the ones who scattered in the panic."

Zebulun was thankful for the distraction and followed another of his brothers to gather the flock together again. He flashed a weak smile Judah's way as he left.

"Good lad," Judah responded. "We don't want to lose any more from falling between the rocks."

"Okay, Judah," Reuben said, once the boy was out of sight. "Let's do this."

Both men drew their knives and finished what the wolves had started by putting the two suffering ewes out of their misery.

"Looks like lamb for dinner tomorrow," Reuben said, a sad sigh blowing through his lips.

"And moving away from this pack's home territory," Judah replied while tying up the dead animals.

"We need to gather the flock first, and allow them to settle," Reuben replied. "We don't want any of these ladies to abort from the fright they've had. We'll stay put tomorrow and move the day after."

III

The sheep had been skittish – the shepherds too.

The disturbance of the previous night had made everyone nervous, and sleep deprivation had made the ten sons of Jacob cranky. Tempers had flared easily, which had done nothing to settle the flock. Reuben had wisely allocated short sleep sessions in pairs for his brothers, while at the same time trying to cover his own anxiety by staying busy.

Now, two decades later, Judah couldn't stop the memories from flooding back. It felt like he had been transported into the past, his tent now filled with the sights, smells, and sounds of everything he had locked up those many years ago. And no amount of shaking his head could stop the torrent of what happened that awful day from overwhelming him. Guilt grew fingers that tightened around Judah's throat. He could barely breathe as the replay of his sin continued.

By noon, the brothers had gathered around the cooking fire, the taste of wolf-slaughtered lamb unpleasant in their mouths. Conversation had dried up following discussion of Reuben's plans for the rest of their stay in Dothan. The distant howling during the night resulted in agreement for once – they would move the flock tomorrow. Maybe even start the journey homeward.

"Oh no," scowled Issachar, dropping his bowl on the ground. "That's all we need!"

Judah turned in the direction of Issachar's sight thinking he'd spotted a wolf. Instead, he saw the hazy shape of a man leading a donkey against the horizon.

"Who could be travelling alone out here?" Reuben queried. "Is he mad? Doesn't he know there are wolves about?"

"Of course he's mad," replied Issachar, "it's Joseph!"

"No, it can't be."

"It is. Don't you see the sun glint on his coloured coat? All the way down to its useless sleeves."

Judah joined in the ripple of laughter as it mixed with the disdain rising like bile in the brothers' throats. Soon the sarcasm turned so sour it filled the air with loathing. Treachery was quickly added to what sounded more like a crowd of bandits than a family of brothers.

"Let's be done with the dreamer once and for all!"

"I'm tired of his arrogance. There'll be no inheritance left for us if Joseph has anything to do with it."

As the lone traveller edged ever closer the rabble-rousers had kindled a fire in the belly of even the quietest among them. And years later Judah could recall every word... every threat... and he could still taste the hatred that had filled their mouths back then.

"Kill him, I say," shouted one, to the cheers and excitement of the others. "We'll never have to listen to his foolishness again ... never again have to watch Father fawn over him and ignore us."

"We can blame the wolves," added another. The very suggestion suddenly making all their threats possible. They could do it. They could kill Joseph and never be suspected. It was a perfect plan. The wolf – their enemy – suddenly became a friend.

Raucous laughter rose into the air in a sign of assent. And as Joseph came closer his fate was sealed by one final comment.

"We can dump his body in that dry well. Let his bones rot! No one will ever find him."

But Reuben wasn't cheering as loudly as the others. His conscience was pricked. They couldn't kill their own brother, no matter how obnoxious they thought his behaviour. As the men he'd stood beside against wolves on the previous night congratulated each other on their plot of fratricide, Jacob's firstborn frantically threw together a plan to save Joseph's life. He didn't like him any more than the others, but he wasn't going to be the one to witness a murder he'd later have to explain to his father by lying.

"Enough! Enough!"

Reuben's words broke through the noise of triumph.

"Joseph is our brother."

Reuben's attempt to speak was met with grumbling and raised fists, but he was having none of it.

"Let's teach him a lesson – yes – but we cannot shed his blood!"

The murmuring continued but Reuben commanded their attention with a raise of his hand. Conversation ceased in respect for their leader. However, his words did nothing to dampen the hatred that had festered for so long in these men who felt threatened by a seventeen-year-old boy.

But they listened, and Reuben thought his suggestion would give him enough time to free Joseph and send him quickly home.

"When we've shown him what we think of him, we can throw him down the well – give him time to reflect on all the trouble he's caused us."

Hatred hung as heavy as the wool on sheep ready for shearing.

"Brothers! Brothers!"

Joseph's enthusiastic call drew growls from the men seated around the fire. Few looked up to see the smile beam across the face of their soon-to-be victim.

"Brothers," called Joseph again, "I've finally found you! I've been searching…"

"Now!" yelled Naphtali.

Joseph dropped the reins of his donkey. Totally unprepared for the attack, he fell backwards with the first blow. Hands pulled at his coat from every angle. He could hear the seams rip as dirt was kicked in his face. Struggling against his attackers, Joseph was powerless against so many. Someone struck his face. Another pulled his hair. Spittle coursed down his cheeks. Many a mock fight they'd had as boys growing up, but this was different. Joseph was terrified.

Faces. He could see their faces. Name their names.

What was happening? Had the sun melted their brains?

"It's – Jo-seph!" He tried to call out, but his words were broken by lack of air. Someone was kneeling on his chest.

"Yo-ur bro-ther!" he gasped.

As blackness enveloped him Joseph could hear Reuben. He wanted to call for help but he couldn't.

"Throw him into the well."

It was Reuben.

Reuben? How could Reuben do this to me?

As his bruised body hit the rubble at the bottom of the well, Joseph succumbed to the darkness, glad of the temporary escape from the unfolding horror.

The memory was all too much for Judah. The vivid flashbacks tore at him like the wolves had savaged the lambs. He ached from head to foot, longing that sleep would take him and calm his troubled soul. How had he kept this secret for so long? Where did he manage to store the horror of his actions all these years? Judah and his brothers had never spoken of it after they presented Jacob with Joseph's bloodied coat. They thought themselves so clever when the broken-hearted Jacob himself declared: "This is my son's coat... he must have been devoured by a wild animal." They didn't even have to lie. They'd got away with it.

What have we done? What have I done? How could I have pretended all these years that Joseph got what he deserved? When did I become such a monster?

The war with guilt waged on in Judah's heart. Sleep would not come while recollections needed to be dragged from his darkened soul. It was time. Time to face what remained of the story.

Reuben had left them eating around the campfire, having gone off to check the far edges of the flock. Judah couldn't help noticing how troubled his older brother had become since Joseph was thrown into the well. His thoughts momentarily left the merriment at Joseph's predicament, recognising that Reuben was going to have to explain Joseph's disappearance to their father. Not a job he himself would like to do.

Suddenly a bundle of cloth struck him in the face, returning Judah from his thoughts. The brightly coloured – now torn – coat belonging to Joseph was doing the rounds of the brothers. Laughter filled the circle as one after another acted out Joseph's earlier dreams, demanding the others bow down in worship before them. Judah joined the mockery, standing to his feet with the robe of his father's favourite wrapped around him.

The sound of drinking, and laughter didn't have to travel far to penetrate the deep stone prison where Joseph lay injured. Yet no shame was felt around the fire.

As a ladle was dipped into the bubbling stew, Judah lifted his eyes to the horizon once again. The distinctive shape of camels came clearly into view. Well laden with goods for the Egyptian market, the caravan was heading in their direction. Midianite traders, Judah reckoned. Wealthy into the bargain. That's when the idea hit him. He thought it might get Reuben out of a spot too.

"Listen, brothers," Judah said, grabbing their attention. "What's the point in killing Joseph? Why not make a little money for our trouble?"

Once money was mentioned Judah had their attention.

"There's a caravan over there. It's heading our way... probably bound for Egypt. Why don't we sell Joseph to the traders? They'll give a good price for him. He's young. Well fed. Muscular."

"What could we make from such a sale?" one of his brothers asked, as though selling your brother was an everyday occurrence.

"I've heard fifteen to thirty shekels is the going rate for young male slaves," Judah replied. "At least this way we won't have to kill him. He is our own flesh and blood after all."

Thinking on his words Judah tried to convince himself that he was saving Joseph from certain death, but somehow it rang hollow.

"Shouldn't we ask Reuben?" Issachar questioned.

"We would if he were here," Judah replied. "But we need to decide quickly, the caravan is almost upon us."

One by one the brothers assented to Judah's plan, the thought of money strengthening their already weak wills. While Judah waved down the caravan driver, the others lowered a rope into the well to pull Joseph up. Poor Joseph. He thought his brothers had finished having fun with him and that he would finally be able to pass on their father's greetings to them. But it was not to be.

"He's worth more," Joseph heard Judah say to the trader. "But we need to settle this… twenty shekels and we have a deal."

Before he could speak, Joseph watched the merchant take twenty pieces of silver from his pouch and pass it to Judah.

I am being sold! By my own brothers!

Panic swept over the seventeen-year-old. He tried pleading. It did no good. No one was listening. Instead, his siblings taunted and laughed at Joseph as his new masters dragged him away to a life of slavery.

"Who's going to bow to you now Joseph?" one of them shouted.

The younger brother turned, his eyes pleading… begging. But even his torturous cries for help carried no persuasion. Joseph was now the property of traders: sellers of gum, balm, myrrh, and now human flesh. And as the Midianites tied the favourite son of Jacob to a camel, the final sound he heard from his brothers was laughter. The one who'd told them he'd dreamt they would all bow down to him one day was going to spend the rest of his life bowing down to others

And Judah, pleased with his bartering skills, smugly divided the silver with his brothers.

Now, weeping in his tent, Judah heard Joseph's cries for the first time. Neither the desire for petty revenge, nor the pressure of sibling rivalry, could block the sound of his young brother's distress from assaulting Judah's conscience any more. The vile truth of the whole sordid affair overwhelmed him. There was no excuse. No reason on earth to justify their – his – actions on that most dreadful of days. He'd sold his own brother as a slave! Then he'd contributed to the lie that broke his father's heart.

Judah was as guilty back then as he was in his despicable treatment of Tamar today… as he continued to be with his father, every time he heard the old man mourn for his dead son.

Guilty.

As the sleepless night crept towards dawn, Judah's broken spirit groaned words of repentance.

"I am sorry, Tamar. I am sorry, Father." His voice, choked with emotion, trembled with his final confession. "And Joseph… I am so, so, sorry. I wish I could go back…"

Wishing couldn't take Judah back… but forgiveness could take him forward. And the God of Heaven heard his words, saw his penitence, and began a change in Judah's heart.

IV

Judah couldn't believe where he was going.

An uncomfortable silence hung like a blanket over the ten brothers as they made the slow trek towards Egypt. Urging empty pack animals along did nothing to speed their journey. The donkeys may have been load-light but each man carried an unimaginable weight in their hearts. Yet none willingly spoke of the last family member to make the journey to Egypt.

Two days earlier, Jacob had summoned his sons to a family meeting. Following the Tamar incident, Judah had visited the family more often, and the pagan temples less. It was Hebrew company he sought more regularly now. That pleased his old father – even if Judah himself found it hard to see the grief lines etched on Jacob's face.

Famine.

That was the reason for the family gathering. Each man gave a sombre account to Jacob of how their families were coping with the blight on their crops. As if that wasn't bad enough, the markets were empty and the traders devoid of foodstuffs to sell. The normal movement of goods had quite simply dried up much like the pasture they needed to feed their sheep. Both land and life were desolate.

"The flocks are decimated Father," Reuben had told Jacob. "It's a pitiful sight watching them starve, but not nearly as sad as watching our children cry themselves to sleep with hungry bellies."

A rumble of assent followed Reuben's comments, with each of Jacob's sons relating personal stories of woe.

"We fear for our children's lives, Father."

Zebulun's words were accompanied by tears that sought refuge in his beard, having watched a family bury their stillborn baby days earlier. Dying lambs were bad enough, but the thought of losing your children to starvation was unthinkable.

Soon everyone was talking over each other. The noise rose to a crescendo before Jacob beat his staff against a nearby log bringing his sons to attention.

"Why are you all looking at one another yet doing nothing about it?" the old man questioned. "You talk as if there's no way out, yet you know full well that there's grain for sale in Egypt."

"Egypt, Father?"

Reuben broke the silence that had overtaken his brothers. The very mention of that place had glued their lips together. It was the place they never spoke of, but it was the only place where they would be able to purchase food for their families. Every country in the region was in the same position as Canaan, yet somehow Egypt had storehouses full of grain. Recently, all roads headed south, but it wasn't just around the corner.

"Egypt? That's a six-week journey Father. It would take months for us to complete the round trip… and we don't even know if the Egyptians will sell their grain to us."

"They might never let us return, Father," interjected Benjamin. "They might make us their slaves."

"You will not be going, Benjamin." Jacob's instant retort causing his youngest son to blush. "I will not lose you too. You will stay here."

"But Father, I am not a child…"

"You are the only child of your mother left to me!" Jacob insisted. "I *cannot* lose you like I lost Joseph."

Reuben placed a hand on Benjamin's shoulder forcing him to sit, a silent shake of the head telling Jacob's youngest not to fight it. As Jacob's oldest son, Reuben had always regretted not returning to the well in time to save Joseph. His life thereafter was dogged by guilt, and dedicated to serving his father, whose grief never lessened. He didn't want to put Benjamin at risk either, as none of them could be sure how this proposed journey might go.

"Father." Judah spoke up this time. "The Egyptians do not like us Hebrews. What if they kill us and none of us return? Who will feed our families then?"

"What is wrong with you all?" Jacob shouted, confused by his sons' response. "You cannot feed your families as it is! Would you have them die of starvation because you refuse to go in search of food? We will not beg! We have money with which to do business with the Egyptians. Of course they will sell you grain."

Fear and guilt do not make good bedfellows. The brothers had good reason to fear the Egyptians, who were suspicious of all things foreign. The possibility of meeting Joseph didn't even cross their minds – he was undoubtedly dead by now. Slaves didn't exactly live a long life, especially in brutal Egypt. However, the thought of making the same journey that Joseph had taken made the brothers' skin crawl. None knew how the other felt, but Judah's recent battle with guilt had taught him that the only way to defeat it was to face it head on, however painful. He was just about to break the uncomfortable silence when his father beat him to it.

"You will go to Egypt," Jacob commanded. "And you will buy food, or we will all die. Get up and make preparations. You leave tomorrow."

The journey was even more difficult than the brothers could have imagined.

The roads were busy, but the usual cheery greetings from travellers were replaced by sad words: each absorbed in their own personal misery. Gaunt faces met them at every turn, while the carcasses of pack animals, too weak to finish the journey, littered the roadside. Judah couldn't watch while locals hacked at what was left of dead donkeys once the vultures had filled their bellies. How had they come to this? Yet it was sights like these that pushed the brothers on, firing determination to bring proper food back to their own families.

As they came closer to their destination Judah noticed that those leaving Egypt looked altogether different. Hope was now written on faces that had arrived etched with pain. Sacks bulged on the backs of mules that had been strengthened with food for the return home. Yet, concern was still visible. How could they pass the starving and keep their load intact? Many, like Judah and his brothers, had come a long way and needed to bring back all the grain they could purchase for their own starving families at home. Yet his heart ached for those around him who would pray for the life of their own children tonight.

"Please have mercy, Jehovah," whispered Judah. "Don't let them starve..."

Reuben's voice intruded on Judah's prayer, summoning his attention. Long lines stretched in front of them. Something ahead had halted the already slow movement towards their journey's end.

"Friend," Reuben called to a fellow Hebrew heading out of Egypt. "What's the hold up on the road?"

"Border checks," came the reply. "You have to register before they allow you into the country.

"You cannot do business with them unless you register and then present the seal given here to the commissioners at the storehouses," the man continued, raising his voice so Reuben could hear above the hubbub. "Tell them only the truth. They are on the lookout for spies."

"Spies?"

"Yes, Zebulun." Reuben turned to answer his brother: "Remember, this is the only land of these many nations that has food. Now would be the perfect time for invasion."

"Who is strong enough to send an army?" Zebulun retorted. "You can't fight on an empty stomach!"

The conversation on politics passed the time as the men waited in line for their turn to be registered. They were shepherds, members of one family, not a military man among them. Surely they would have no problems getting through? Once family details were recorded and money had changed hands, the band of brothers were given directions as to where they could buy the precious cargo they'd come for. They had another few miles to go, but at least they could now buy bread to quiet their rumbling stomachs.

Bread never tasted so good; the ten brothers tucked in after finding a secluded place in the corner of the market square. Judah was glad of the privacy as they stuffed their faces in the most unmannerly way... but he was wrong. Lifting his head momentarily, he jumped at the sight of the little group of children who'd gathered around them.

Dumbstruck, Judah tapped Reuben's leg. There in front of them stood four little boys – completely naked! Their heads were shaved apart from one strange lock of plaited hair falling from the crown of their head and down over one ear. Thick, black, almond-shaped markings spread around their eyes, while their wrists and ankles jangled at even the most imperceptible movement. Only the tallest of the boys wore a yellow-metal collar around his neck, and he couldn't have been more than six years old.

The boys looked horrified, gazing at Judah and his brothers as if they were monsters. Then the youngest of the children started to cry, wailing as he hid behind one whom they guessed was his brother. Reuben made a move to calm the child, terrified that the boy's crying might bring trouble their way. One move was all it took. In a flash they were gone, no doubt with a story to tell about the strange men who wore robes as long as women and had hair growing all over their heads and faces.

Reuben took no time in getting them on their way once more. He couldn't risk the commotion landing them in prison. The city of On was close by. The sooner they completed their business, the sooner they'd leave this pagan land behind. Judah agreed. Everywhere they looked literally teemed with partially clothed men, seductive women covered in ornamented jewellery, and naked slaves working in the fields.

Had these people no shame?

To make matters worse, as they entered the great city of On – centre of worship to the sun god, Ra – they were overwhelmed by the trappings of idol worship. Soldier-like statues lined the streets – gold-painted bodies of men with hawk heads – each one topped with a solar disk. It was terrifying, made worse by the shadow of an immeasurable obelisk falling on them as they approached the Temple of Atum.

"Do you know where you are going, Reuben?" asked Issachar, disturbed by the chanting emanating from the temple.

"We've to take the road to the right of the temple. Apparently, we are to meet the governor at his office."

"The governor... of all Egypt? Does he not have commissioners to do his work for him?"

"It seems we are among the privileged few. We will conduct our business with the governor himself," replied Reuben, not wanting to appear nervous.

But Judah didn't feel privileged. Something wasn't quite right.

V

"You are spies! You have come to find our weaknesses and plan an invasion!"

Judah couldn't believe what he was hearing. Bowed low, with their faces all but pressed into the marble floor, Zaphnath-Paaneah towered above them: regal, almost god-like. His fine clothing, complete with gold chain resting on his bare muscular chest and ornate gold bracelets stretching up his forearms, served only to remind the men from Canaan of their lowly status in life. Thankfully the governor's servants had brought them water to wash in before returning them to the judgment hall after they had spent three days locked up.

But nothing had changed. Four times Zaphnath-Paaneah had accused them of being spies. Each time, Reuben had replied with the same responses.

"Sir, we are your servants – we are honest men, not spies!"

Judah cringed at Reuben's description of them as 'honest' men.

"We are simply twelve brothers," Reuben pleaded. "The sons of one old man in the land of Canaan. Ten of us came to bring back food to our starving families, while our youngest brother stayed with our father... and..." he hesitated, "one is no longer with us."

"Prove your honesty or you will all die. Do what I ask and you shall live, for I fear God," the governor replied. The men rose from the floor, hope rising as the Egyptian continued. "One of you will stay here, imprisoned, while the rest of you return with food for your families. You will then come back to me and bring your youngest brother with you. Then, and only then, will I believe that you are honest men."

And still they didn't recognise the man to whom they had bowed.

Instead, they huddled together to discuss the governor's demands, while he sat back on his throne. The choice presented was no choice at all. They had to agree. One of them had to remain in prison if they were to bring home any food. But each man knew there was no way that Jacob would ever allow Benjamin to come back to Egypt with them. Panic began to set in, loosening tongues that had been tied for two decades.

"You know what's happening here?" said Issachar.

"Yes. We're not fools!" replied Zebulun.

One after another, they owned up to their guilt over what they did to Joseph – not realising he was only a few feet away.

"We listened to him cry... and we laughed."

"We sat eating... while he languished in the well, pleading for a drink."

"He begged us..."

"And we mocked him."

"And I sold my own brother for twenty shekels," Judah added. "Sold him into slavery... a horrific existence... an early death."

"If this man knew what we had done, he would know we were not honest men."

"And if you'd done what I'd told you we'd not be in this predicament. I told you not to sin against the boy," Reuben interjected. "Now we are being judged for Joseph's blood."

"And we are guilty," Judah responded.

But the man on the throne did know what they had done; he did know the pain they had caused, the rejection he had suffered. But he was not dead. Joseph was very much alive and living out the dreams given to him as a boy. He had recognised his brothers the very moment they'd stepped in front of him three days earlier. An interpreter was not needed to hear their confession, although the brothers did not know that. But their confession sent him from their presence to weep in private. Perhaps they had become honest men after all. He'd give them a chance... something they hadn't done for him.

Judah noticed that the governor had left them, thinking he'd gone to see to some other business. When he returned, the brothers had a decision for him. They would do as he asked.

Who could they choose to stay behind? How could they choose?

But that was one decision they didn't have to make. With a stretch of his long arm the Egyptian pointed directly at Simeon. He would be the one to stay behind. As quickly as a gasp left their lips, Simeon was taken away by two strong guards. A hurried glance over his shoulder allowed the captive what might be the last sight he'd ever have of his brothers.

"Don't worry, Simeon," called Judah as his brother was dragged through a door. "We'll be back... I prom... ise." But his final words bounced back off the wood. And when he turned around Zaphnath-Paaneah was nowhere to be seen.

VI

While the stack of bread grew smaller at each meal in Jacob's home, the famine raged on, showing no sign of abating. It was happening exactly as the Egyptians had said, and if they were right, it had years yet to run.

"It's time for you to return to Egypt," Jacob said to his sons as they sat around the fire. "We need to buy more food."

Each looked at the other exasperated, having brought up this subject so many times over the intervening months. But it was Judah who replied, voicing the facts to the old man yet again.

"Don't you get it, Father? We cannot return to Egypt without Benjamin. The governor was adamant."

The others nodded in agreement, a few commenting to reinforce Judah's response.

"Remember what we told you, Father. He won't even see us if our youngest brother is not with us. And all this time Simeon is languishing in prison, wondering if we will ever return to bring him home."

"Why did you tell him you had another brother? How could you be so cruel to me?"

Jacob's self-pity was pathetic. His fear of losing Benjamin trumped any concern over the others in his large family – including Simeon, and the grandchildren who played at his feet. It appeared he'd rather see them all starve before risking Benjamin's life. It was the Joseph situation all over again – favouritism, Jacob's tarnished badge of fatherhood. But this time Judah was having none of it.

"If we hadn't wasted all this time, we could have been to Egypt and back twice!"

Whether it was Judah's promise of taking personal responsibility for Benjamin's safety, or an unspoken admission of wrong, Jacob said an emotional goodbye to his sons. But not before insisting they pack a generous gift for the man who held all of their futures in his hands. Then, in an attempt to cover all eventualities, Jacob doubled the money required, to ensure they could repay what was found in their sacks when they returned home last time.

That issue alone filled the brothers with dread. Would they be seen, and consequently punished, as thieves once they crossed the Egyptian border? Judah had no idea how the money had got back into their sacks after they had paid for the grain. But he was sure of one thing, it would be hard enough to explain to friends, never mind suspicious foreigners. He sighed as the silhouette of his father faded into the hazy horizon behind them, and repeated Jacob's prayer as the band of brothers headed cross-country to meet the Way of the Sea.

"God Almighty grant us mercy before the man, and may we return safely with Simeon and Benjamin."

Judah and Reuben walked together on the long, dusty road. Each lost in their own thoughts and fears. There was so much more at stake than food. Since they'd last been in Egypt, the brothers often talked of their experiences; of the harsh way the governor spoke to them; of the three nights they'd spent in prison; of saying goodbye to Simeon.

"Do you think Simeon is okay, Reuben?"

"I think so, Judah. At least I hope so."

"Why didn't you push Father much sooner than this? We should have left weeks ago."

This time the question came from an eavesdropper to the older brothers' conversation.

"Because of you, Benjamin," Judah snapped. "Father wouldn't see reason... not when all he could see was you."

"It wasn't my fault," Benjamin defended. "Honestly, I pleaded with him many times to let me go with you. He wouldn't listen. I'm worried about Simeon too."

"I know, Benjamin," Judah replied, softening. "That wasn't fair... blaming you. It's just that..."

"Father's never been the same since Joseph died."

Joseph.

Judah sighed at the mention of his name, wondering how different they all would have been if he hadn't sold his brother as a slave.

"He still has the coat, you know."

"What?"

"Father," Benjamin replied. "He still has that bloodstained coloured coat hidden away in the sack at the back of his tent."

"I don't believe you, Benjamin," Reuben interjected. "Why would father ever keep that torn, bloodied, smelly thing?"

"Because he is a father," Judah said, uncomfortable with the conversation. "And probably because the last time he saw Joseph, he was wearing it."

Judah hoped that would be the end of the conversation, but how wrong he was.

"Do you think he's still alive?" Benjamin asked. "Joseph, I mean."

If the ground had opened up, and the sky had fallen in, the question would not have surprised them less.

"Of course not, Benjamin!" Reuben gasped. "You saw the coat. Joseph is dead, and that's an end of it!"

"But…"

"Enough, Benjamin… no more."

But as the young man slipped back to join the others, Judah's heart sank, weighed once more by guilt from long ago.

"Joseph," he whispered, as the sun started to sink in the western sky.

On this occasion Reuben had chosen a different route to Egypt. The Way of the Sea was cooler, but he'd also hoped to encounter fewer harrowing scenes than on the rural roads they'd travelled before.

Wrong again.

Scavengers were the only creatures that had meat on their bones. Fields were bare; homes crumbling; people carried with them the look of death… and beggars lined the roads where flowers once grew. Even Benjamin learned quickly to keep his gaze focused on the road ahead. But averting his eyes from the desolate sights helped no one, least of all himself.

The sky they travelled beneath may have been blue; the sun beating on them a brilliant yellow; but nature's brushstrokes were only black. Colour had been stolen from the land. Every blade of grass had wizened; every leaf had fallen; each man, woman, and child sitting at the side of the road was as lifeless as the landscape around them.

Dreary days passed too slowly into weeks until, finally, the brothers spotted the crowds ahead. Waiting. Waiting to be let into the land of plenty – the breadbasket of the world. But in the hearts of the sons of Jacob, fear rose as they waited in line. They'd planned their strategy, rehearsed their speeches, and as they reached the Egyptian border post the brothers closed around Benjamin with the kind of protection they'd never afforded his full brother.

"*Adonai*, have mercy," Judah whispered, only too aware that he wasn't the only one praying.

Reuben stepped forward to register the family and to seek permission to buy grain. This time he asked for an audience with Zaphnath-Paaneah, explaining that the governor had asked them to see him on their return. While Reuben was still speaking, Judah noticed one of the guards jump on a horse and leave the post.

We've been found out, Judah thought. They know about the money! Soon we'll be in prison with Simeon.

Surrounded once again by a culture totally foreign in every way was only slightly easier the second time round. But they weren't the only strangers filling Egypt's cities. It seemed the world wandered the streets, much to the amusement of the local children who couldn't understand why the foreigners all wore so many clothes.

This time they went straight to the governor's office, but they didn't make it across the threshold. Blocking the door stood the governor's steward, as broad as he was tall. The servant looked like a wildcat ready to attack – the kohl around his eyes blacker than before, lined with a translucent green – and they felt easy prey.

"You have returned," he said. Stating the obvious did not calm their racing hearts. "I have been commanded to bring you to my master's house. Please, follow me."

The governor's house! Judah was in the same state of panic as the rest of them. How will I be able to protect Benjamin there? What does the Egyptian want with us? He obviously knows about the money.

"What does he want with us?" asked a nervous Benjamin, coming up alongside Judah. "Will he make us all his servants, Judah?"

"I don't know, Benjamin, but you must stay behind me... hide among us." Judah's reply was meant to calm the youngest, but it only served to raise his anxiety further.

"What does he want with me, Judah? Why did the governor ask for me?"

"This is only a headcount, Benjamin – proof that we told him the truth when we were here before."

"But now that the man thinks you are thieves, what will he do now?"

Benjamin's whispering echoed the very thoughts of Judah's heart. On this occasion they were not guilty. But then neither was Joseph when he sold him to the Midianites.

Arriving at the door of Zaphnath-Paaneah's house, Judah and the nine were so distressed that they couldn't hold the secret of the money any longer. Thinking perhaps that the governor's steward might know their fate, the men blurted out their fears. The servant listened to them rehearse how they had found the grain payment back in their sacks following their first visit. With an unexpected softness in his facial expression, the servant looked at them as if this news was not worthy of either his concern, or theirs.

"Don't worry," he replied. "There's no need to be afraid. I received payment for your grain." With a shrug of his broad shoulders he continued, "It must have been God – the God of your father – who put the treasure in your sacks." And with that he clapped his hands loudly, summoning others from the house. As the beasts were led away to be fed, the steward suddenly appeared with Simeon!

The reunion was both chaotic and emotional. There were hugs and tears in abundance when the brothers were reunited. As Judah embraced Simeon, a thought flitted across his mind.

How did the steward know that Benjamin was with them?

Once inside the grand residence, water was brought to Judah and his brothers so that they could refresh themselves. Could this day get any better? Would Zaphnath-Paaneah be as easily persuaded as his steward? The answer shot across their silent questions instantly.

"The master will feast with you at noon," the steward said, as if it was something the second most powerful man in all of Egypt did every day. "Please prepare yourselves to meet with him." And then he left.

It took a short time for the information to sink in as the noisy reunion with Simeon continued in a flood of questions and general hysteria.

"Feast?"

Reuben's one word silenced the room.

"Zaphnath-Paaneah is hosting a feast for us! Hebrews? I thought the Egyptians didn't like herdsmen... especially Hebrew shepherds."

"You are right, Reuben," interrupted Zebulun. "You see the way the locals look at us in the market. Why on earth would he want to eat with us?"

"What does it matter?" shouted another. "Free food sounds good to me."

Laughter filled the room. Something Judah hadn't heard in a long time.

Perhaps God has heard our prayer after all, he mused, as he and Reuben made ready the gifts Jacob had sent for Egypt's governor.

VII

Fine, brightly coloured linens draped the walls of the long meeting room into which the brothers were shown. Statues covered in gold stood majestically on carved stone pedestals. Fresh flowers added beauty to a place that required no further adornment, yet their presence reminded the brothers how long it had been since any such delight had grown in their drought-ridden homeland.

Judah's hand pushed Benjamin towards the floor as Zaphnath-Paaneah entered the room. After Reuben presented the gifts, he joined his brothers in deference – all eleven bowed low. They'd barely raised their heads again when the governor started asking after their father's health. The men were keen to show their respect to Zaphnath-Paaneah, and quickly dropped to the floor again – this time prostrating themselves before the Egyptian. They couldn't risk further accusations of spying, or theft, hence the keenness with which they grovelled.

The governor's words – always through an interpreter – brought them nervously to their knees once more.

"So, this is your youngest brother?" he said, pointing out Benjamin. "May God be gracious to you, my son!" And as fast as the words had left his mouth, the man rushed from the room as though a scorpion had bitten him.

"Don't you find his words strange, Reuben?" Judah asked. "Why does he seek a blessing from God for Benjamin? Which god does he invoke? There's no mention of Ra from his lips. You would almost think he was speaking of the God of our fathers, and not his own."

"You think too much, Judah. I've heard he has a cup of divination and by it he knows all kind of things."

"Serve the food!"

The command signalled the governor's return, while the anticipation of a meal rather than an enquiry about money was very welcome. Servants directed the guests to the far end of the hall where low tables had been set, seating each man according to the order of their birth.

"How does he know this?" Levi whispered to Judah. "Do you see what he's done?"

"Of course, I…"

"Magic," interrupted Dan, from Judah's other side.

"Quiet, Dan. Do you want us all killed?"

But Judah couldn't get the thought to leave him. How did this man know so much about them? With so many strangers in front of him every day, how did he manage to pick out Benjamin so easily from the rest of his brothers? From where he sat, Judah watched Zaphnath-Paaneah sit alone as the food was served. The rest of his entourage sat at another table. On this occasion, it was clear that Egyptians didn't eat with Hebrews, neither did leaders eat with servants. As Judah ate with his brothers, Egypt's second ruler cut a lonely figure.

Excited voices rose from the Hebrew table, like children at a party. The food had arrived! Each man had a golden platter set in front of him. Fish, goat, beef, green-shooted onions, garlic, and cucumber filled every plate. Foods they couldn't name sat alongside those they hadn't seen for over two years since the famine began. Bread enough for a family was portioned to each of them, while their cups were filled with beer... again and again.

And the laughter from the end of the table drew in those seated opposite, as no less than five platters were sat in front of Benjamin!

"Feeling hungry, Benjamin?" joked one.

"How come you're the favourite?" teased another.

Benjamin caught Judah's eye with a 'I don't know what's going on' look of surprise, as he literally dived into the food mountain.

As lunch stretched into afternoon, the men feasted and the beer carried away their inhibitions until they hadn't a care in the world.

VIII

"I am Joseph... your brother."

Judah's head spun as if it would leave his shoulders: the whole family of brothers shocked into silence. Having already dropped to their knees, the eleven prostrated themselves, wishing the ground would suck them in.

They had been found out. Their sin was now open for all to see. The festering sore of guilt no longer hidden.

Judah dared not lift his head, the long-ago cries of the young Joseph pleading for mercy screamed in his memory. Yet, they... no, he... had granted Joseph none.

The last twenty-four hours had gone from the sublime to the ridiculous. One minute they had been feasting with the man they knew as Zaphnath-Paaneah, Pharaoh's number two. But suddenly they were being chased by the Palace Guard who accused them of stealing the personal divining cup of the governor.

The threats of imprisonment, slavery, and even death for the perpetrator of the crime seemed reasonable enough. Judah knew the silver cup would never be found in their belongings. The governor had been good to them. They would never repay him by stealing.

Judah watched the guards go through their bags – from the oldest brother to the youngest – in order. Judah breathed easier as each search revealed nothing, apart from money in their sacks as before. He remembered thinking that someone was playing tricks on them.

Then it was Benjamin's turn. Though he was shaken by the whole experience, he was simply expecting to follow what the others had experienced. So when the guard pulled the missing silver cup from his sack, the colour drained from the youngest brother's face.

"I did not do this, Judah," he cried. "Truthfully. I did not do this."

Now back in the very place where they had feasted on the day before, their terror was tangible. This powerful man was threatening to make Benjamin his slave! What kind of a sick joke was this? How could they return home without Benjamin? It would kill their father. In the panic now devouring Judah, he made a final, personal plea to the man he himself had sold into slavery.

I will not be responsible depriving Jacob of another son.

In what can only be described as Judah's finest moment, he opened his heart to this stranger. And out it all came. The story of a man with a favourite wife, who bore him two sons that he loved with all his heart. One of those sons had left one day never to return – their father believed him dead – torn to pieces by a wild animal. Judah vividly explained how it broke the old man's heart, leaving him never the same again.

He was too intent on finishing his speech to notice the powerful man was trembling. He continued his plea, explaining how their families were starving back home, how they'd begged their father to let them come back to Egypt with Benjamin or they would all die.

"But God has found us out. He knows we are guilty," Judah declared, causing a stir in the room.

Guilty!

Yet only the Egyptians in the room did not realise that the guilt Judah confessed had nothing to do with a silver cup.

"Please, my Lord, I beg of you, take me as your servant in place of Benjamin. For if we do not bring him home our father will surely die."

Suddenly the governor screamed, not for their blood, but for the room to be cleared of his staff, who scurried off like rats deserting a sinking ship.

Was he going to kill them himself?

But before the thought had time to form properly in Judah's mind, Zaphnath-Paaneah was the one on his knees... weeping. The sound of his crying filled the room, piercing through the walls. He was beyond distressed, as if years of tears needed to be spilt in one torrential flood. His shoulders heaved, attempting to offload the burdens of his past.

Judah fell to the floor again beside his brothers. They didn't know what to do: didn't know what to think. Had the man lost his mind?

Then Zaphnath-Paaneah composed himself and spoke – his voice shook but the words were clear... and in Hebrew!

"I am Joseph!" he blurted out. "Is my father really alive?"

Joseph?!

No. It can't be true! Joseph is dead!

Shock. Disbelief. Horror. Disgrace. Fear. Terror. Every negative emotion known to man welled up in ten of the eleven hearts bowed before... Joseph. But if the servants had returned, it would have been guilt that met them at the door. The guilty ones trembled in front of their father's favourite son – the brother they had wronged twenty-two years earlier. Joseph, whom they'd despised so much that they'd wished, even planned, his death.

"We deserve to die," Judah whispered.

Yet despite the blanket of fear that had fallen with Joseph's words, the brothers heard him call to them.

"Get up," he was saying. "Get up. Come closer, please."

As they rose from their place of shame and shuffled closer, none dared lift their head to face him. Hebrew flowed from Joseph's mouth in words of forgiveness and kindness.

"Don't be distressed," he said. "There's no need to be angry with yourselves for your past deeds."

What is he talking about? Judah thought. We sold him! Wished him dead! Lied to our father! Lied to ourselves that we were better off without him!

"You might have sold me here, but God sent me to Egypt to save lives... and to preserve our family for future generations.

"Are you listening to me?" he urged, his voice stronger now. "It was God who made me lord of Pharaoh's house and ruler of all Egypt."

Judah dared to lift his head and before him stood the now grown-up teenager of their childhood. The dreamer had become a prince: the leader of millions, the saviour of the destitute, the one to whom the whole world bowed. And now Joseph – brother Joseph – stood taller than the obelisk of On in his willingness to reconcile with those who had done him such wrong.

How can he not hate us?

Yet Joseph's own words had already answered Judah's question.

"It was God..."

It all began to make sense. *Joseph had a right to wear the coat Jacob had given him.* Joseph was never meant to be a shepherd. He was born to be a leader. Isn't that what the dreams were all about? God was trying to prepare them for the day when they would rightly bow down to their brother. The seemingly arrogant boy was destined to become Zaphnath-Paaneah – the man who would save millions from starvation... including his own family.

It was God... but I was too full of jealousy to hear God speak. Too full of pride to see the truth. Too full of hatred to recognise that God had a plan to give Jacob's sons a future.

Judah was spending too much time with memories. Joseph was still speaking, asking them to go home and bring Jacob, along with all their kin, back to Egypt. Judah could hardly keep up with what was happening. There was land already set aside for them to live out the rest of the famine close to Joseph. Promises of housing, food, and all they'd ever need if only they'd tell his father that he was still alive and well... and longing to see him again.

"Surely you can recognise me?" Joseph said. "Benjamin? You know it's me – Joseph – speaking to you?"

And as Joseph embraced his young brother they wept in each other's arms. The reunion melting away the years of separation. When Joseph finally let Benjamin go, he turned to the others and kissed each one of those who had wronged him. Judah thought his heart would break from the guilt he carried, when Joseph pulled him into an embrace.

"I'm sorry, Joseph. I'm sorry," was all he could say.

"It's okay, Judah," Joseph replied, drawing the man who had sold him close to his heart. "It was God who sent me here. You were just part of the plan."

As Judah loosened his hold on Joseph, he sensed that God hadn't finished with him yet. The road to forgiveness involved more than Joseph. An old man sat at home waiting for eleven sons to return. Only God could give Judah the strength to tell Jacob the truth, and only God could give Jacob the grace to forgive him and his brothers. But on that day, in the home of an Egyptian governor, Judah saw in the face of Joseph that forgiveness was possible.

Once the plans for relocation were made, the twelve sat talking of home and family… as brothers do.

Adapted from the story of Judah as told in Genesis 37, 38, 42–45.

Guilt: Life lessons

The struggle

Guilt is no stranger to any of us.

It is defined as a state or condition of wrongdoing. In a court of law, a trial determines the guilt or innocence of the one accused of a crime. The person is first given the opportunity to plead 'guilty' or 'not guilty'. If they own up to their guilt, or are found guilty by a jury, then a judge determines how they should be punished for their offence. Setting aside what is required to prove such a verdict, the result is that a wrongdoing has been determined. In this situation, the guilty person does not have to admit, or even feel guilty. He has been found out. He *is* guilty. Wrongdoing always has consequences.

The Bible states that we are all guilty before God: "For all have sinned and fall short of the glory of God" (Romans 3:23). But it also assures us that while we deserve punishment – "The wages of sin is death" (Romans 6:23) – "There is therefore now no condemnation for those who are in Christ Jesus" (Romans 8:1). It is good to remind ourselves that while no one is free from the guilty verdict of sin, Christ has taken our punishment by His death on the cross. We can avail of a full pardon by trusting in Him for, "If we confess our sins, he is faithful and just to forgive us our sins and to cleanse us from all unrighteousness" (1 John 1:9). In this case, it is the Holy Spirit who arouses guilt, or conviction of sin as some call it, which starts us on the road to repentance.

However, you don't have to be found out to be guilty. Even those of us who have already dealt with the original sin issue by repentance and faith have situations and circumstances that result in guilt. Guilt – whether real or imagined – has a way of embedding itself in our souls. It shows itself not as a fact in a trial, but as a feeling. And it is one emotion that cannot be suppressed indefinitely. Hiding it away is unhealthy and can be destructive.

God uses these guilty feelings to show us our sin. Yet to feel we have done something wrong does not always lead to a desire to put it right. That requires remorse – sorrow towards the person we have wronged.

Our guilt needs to be made personal. Not just a memory of the thing we have done, but a recognition of the hurt caused. Until that happens both parties will suffer. Remorse is more powerful than guilt. It seeks confession and can lead to repentance and reconciliation.

That's what happened to Judah. A close look at his actions since the Joseph incident (Genesis 37:23–28) clearly shows he had felt guilty since the day he had returned home and witnessed his father's grief (Genesis 37:34–35). Then when he was confronted with his sin against Tamar (Genesis 38:25), his guilt was compounded and he finally began to feel remorse (Genesis 38:26). Now it was no longer the act of selling his brother, or of prostituting his daughter-in-law, that was the cause of Judah's inner turmoil, it was the pain he had inflicted on three individuals. His guilt bore the image of three faces – Joseph, Jacob, and Tamar.

Recognising this was the turning point in Judah's life. It was a beginning to putting right the wrongs of his past, which would eventually result in freedom from the tormenting guilt that dogged his life.

It's exactly the same for us. The guilt we feel needs to identify as more than a wrong *act*, there should be a face to it. Our past behaviour involves a person, or people. Identifying the sin and acknowledging the hurt caused is the essence of remorse. And remorse is where the journey to healing can begin.

Stages

The stages of grief are well documented and recognised. Guilt, however, has its own stages or patterns and, like grief, not every stage may be visited but many are. How we handle this has a bearing on how we come out the other side. Guilt can affect our physical, mental, and spiritual health, from symptoms such as indigestion and insomnia, to depression, and even backsliding. Thankfully it also can produce in us a godly sorrow that leads to repentance (2 Corinthians 7:10), and an opportunity to make things right with the person we have wronged. Until that happens we might find ourselves down any or all of these paths...

- **Hide**: There seems to be an instant go-to built into our psyche that encourages us to hide our mistakes. The idea of "if no one else knows, then I haven't done anything wrong" has long been proven a fallacy.

There is always Another who sees; the One whom John reminds us "knows everything" (1 John 3:20), as Adam and Eve discovered (Genesis 3:7–11). Apart from which our own conscience will not let us easily forget what we have done. We might have a certain degree of success in a cover-up but there is no escaping the truth in the words of Numbers 32:23, "be sure your sin will find you out". There really is nowhere to hide.

- **Blame-shifting:** If we've kept our wrongdoing hidden, then blame becomes a game of solitaire, where we make excuses to ourselves to negate our guilt. Conversely, if we are being accused by others, it's an attempt to take the attention off ourselves by shifting the blame elsewhere. *It's their fault, not mine!* Judah was an expert at pointing the finger especially where his family were concerned.

Genetics do play a part in our behaviour. You only have to look at a child often enough to recognise the family 'walk', 'laugh', or 'special ability' for music or sport, etc. However, when we consider moral behaviour, we each have a choice as to whether or not we follow in the footsteps of our nearest and dearest.

There was a long history of deception in Judah's family history. Judah's father Jacob deceived his father Isaac into giving him the blessing of the firstborn that should have gone to Esau (Genesis 27:1–35) – a deception initiated by Judah's grandmother Rebekah. Jacob himself was then deceived into marrying Leah (Genesis 29:25) instead of Rachel by Judah's grandfather Laban and Leah herself. In spite of the example set by senior family members, there is no textual evidence that Judah blamed anyone else for his own deceit over what happened to Joseph.

However, the opportunity for attributing blame came down a different route for Judah. Jacob's favouritism of Joseph over his other eleven sons (Genesis 37:3) sowed hatred in Judah's heart that led to his despicable behaviour against his own brother (Genesis 37:26ff). While we might agree with Judah in our judgment of Jacob's parenting skills, we do well to remember that each of us is responsible for our own actions (Romans 14:12). Judah's sinful response cannot be excused because of his father's foolishness. When we point a finger at someone else there are more pointing back at us.

What a salutary warning to all parents. We stoke trouble and heartache if we follow Jacob's example. Instead, let's remember Paul's words to the believers in Rome: "For God does not show favouritism" (Romans 2:11 NIV). Neither should we.

- **Excuse**: If we still cannot rid ourselves of the guilt, then we might resort to excusing our behaviour by attempting to explain it away. Plausible reasons compete to vindicate our actions, even going as far as to stretch the truth.

"It would never have happened if...", and we add whatever might work best to rationalise what we have done.

You can easily imagine Judah's train of thought over the years. "If my father hadn't made Joseph his favourite, made the rest of us look like fools, had that stupid coat made, kept Joseph at home when the rest of us had to work..." Or: "If only Joseph hadn't played the favourite son, stood up to our father, hadn't told us about his dreams, hadn't worn that stupid coat... then maybe I wouldn't have hated him so much, maybe I wouldn't have sold him, maybe he would still be here... Maybe it would never have happened if..." 'If only' is the devil's torment of the soul.

Don Straka comments: "Situations do not cause people to sin; we choose to sin. Circumstances do not force us to sin. They only help to reveal our sin. No matter how much the cards may seem stacked against us, our sin is always a choice we make."[5]

1 John 1:8 backs that up by reminding us: "If we say we have no sin, we deceive ourselves, and the truth is not in us" – there is simply no excuse.

- **Escape**: Unfortunately, there are those who attempt to escape the feelings of guilt by immersing themselves in some form of addictive behaviour. It can manifest in habits as diverse as overworking to avoid spending too much time with troubling thoughts, right through to the damaging behaviour of alcohol or drug abuse. If you recognise yourself in this, ask God to point out where the real problem is. You may have been successful at hiding what ails you after all, so please seek help.

Guilt is designed to lead to the positive outcome of resolution. Adversely, it can lead to feelings of shame, which is an internalising of your feelings that can result in self-destructive attitudes and actions.

Shame says, "I hate myself" rather than, "I hate what I have done". It is generally acknowledged that shame has strong links with addiction. Perhaps you need to hear again the words of Romans 5:8, "God shows his love for us in that while we were still sinners, Christ died for us". God does not hate us when we go wrong. He loves us unconditionally in spite of our sin. Those feelings of guilt we experience are God's way of pointing us towards the only way of true escape, where we find freedom through confession and forgiveness.

Conscience

God created within all of us a moral awareness of what is right and wrong, including the faculty for self-evaluation. The Apostle Paul writes that even those who know nothing of God's law "demonstrate that God's law is written in their hearts, for their own conscience and thoughts either accuse them or tell them they are doing right" (Romans 2:14–15 NLT). God's desire to make this self-evaluation available to everyone, enables even the most biblically illiterate to discern right from wrong. As Paul says, God's law is written in their hearts.

The conscience is the means God uses to achieve this important response. It is the inner voice or feeling that acts as a guide to help us conform to our value system. When we do what we believe to be right the conscience produces an affirmation of pleasure. When our actions violate the standards we aspire to, then feelings of guilt result (Genesis 42:21). Unfortunately, the conscience is only as strong as the person's value system. A weak value system will produce a weak conscience, while a strong understanding of right and wrong produces a heightened response to our thoughts and actions. That is especially true when our values are based on what the Bible teaches.

However, it needs to be said that the conscience is not infallible. If we set a flawed value system, whether by ignorance or incorrect teaching, then the conscience will neither reward nor challenge us correctly. Too many people carry unnecessary burdens of guilt, and subsequent distress, because the standards by which they measure themselves are wrong. The advice and opinions of others need to be ratified by Scripture before we can follow their lead and allow our conscience to act upon it. That only happens as we mature spiritually through the study and application of God's Word. Then, little by little, God sets the bar for us, enabling us to set our value system correctly.

So, if you are feeling guilty, don't automatically assume the accusation is correct until you examine both the situation and your own heart before the Lord. The same action applies if you are feeling smug about something you have said or done.

"Conscience is a trustworthy guide only when it is informed and ruled by God."[6]

Choices

How did Judah get himself into such a mess? How did things get so bad that he hated his own brother so much that he sold him off as a slave? When his father was in such distress all those years, believing that Joseph was dead, why did Judah not tell him the truth? Why did he lie to Tamar when he had no intention of her marrying his third son? Why did he seek out a prostitute? Why did he consider Tamar's sin as worse than his own? It's no wonder Judah was tormented by guilt with all of that stuffed inside. But it all begs the question I asked earlier. How did Judah get himself into such a mess?

Why did he make the choices he did?

Why do we make the choices we do?

While we can never blame our circumstances for the wrongs we commit, it's helpful to examine situations where our conscience may be dulled, and our reasoning clouded. It's always important to learn from our mistakes and to do all we can not to repeat them.

- **Family**: Our family situation helps to set the value system our conscience will respond to. Healthy, happy families with strong parental role models add to our inbuilt awareness of right and wrong from an early age. Equally, dysfunctional families often offer poor examples of behaviour to build on, both in childhood and beyond. Living in an environment of anger, bitterness, neglect, rejection, compared to one of love, acceptance, affirmation, encouragement, makes an immense difference in how we see ourselves and how we treat others.

  Yet, we don't get to choose our family.

  There is no doubt that Judah was born into a dysfunctional family. His father had four wives, twelve sons, and one daughter – resulting in family politics like no other. In an age when a man's inheritance belonged to the firstborn son, with minor concessions to the rest of his family, it didn't help for the father to show favouritism to a son way down in the pecking order. Jacob was asking for trouble, adding to sibling rivalry that was already rife, to say nothing of his personal history of deceit. What chance did Judah have of making the right decisions in this chaos?

But our circumstances do not determine our behaviour. Reuben grew up in the same family yet he chose not only to do Joseph no harm, but had planned to rescue him (Genesis 37:21, 22). Each of us knows someone who had a difficult start in life yet who overcame it by the choices they made. Others had remarkable privileges early on, with godly parents rooting for them all the way, yet they choose a sinful path no one could have foreseen.

To a certain degree, family life can make us, or sadly, break us, but we alone are responsible for the choices we make (Ezekiel 18:20).

- **Church**: Remarkably, we who belong to Christ have another family to whom we can look for help in setting our value system – the family of God. Church is when family get together, which can happen in a variety of different settings. But within this special family, there are members who are mature and wise, fellowshipping alongside those who are young in the faith and in need of guidance. We need to be looking out for each other. That might mean demonstrating what a real family looks like to those who haven't had the privileges some of us have enjoyed. It is also a challenge to live according to God's Word as others are watching. Our words, attitudes, actions, and reactions might be the lead someone else follows; might be the value system they choose to adopt whether we want them to or not.

God's Word has much to say about the passing on, and receiving, of biblical wisdom and encouragement. In his first letter to the young church at Thessalonica, Paul writes, "Brothers and sisters, we urge you to warn those who are lazy. Encourage those who are timid. Take tender care of those who are weak. Be patient with everyone" (1 Thessalonians 5:14 NLT). Also, the writer to the Hebrews encourages us to be involved in finding ways to help each other become the people we ought to be, "Let us think of ways to motivate one another to acts of love and good works. And let us not neglect our meeting together, as some people do, but encourage one another, especially now that the day of his return is drawing near" (Hebrews 10:24–25 NLT).

- **Friends**: We often look at peer pressure as an issue exclusively for the young when it comes to making life choices. That couldn't be further from the truth. Whatever our age, the pressure to conform to our contemporaries is strong and is high on the blame list when it comes to the choices we make. So concerned are parents that their offspring keep good company that a lot of effort is expended into arranging playdates or activities for our children with those deemed 'suitable' and where it's hoped they'll make the 'right' kind of friends.

Unfortunately, as adults, we are often blinded to the peer pressure we accept, which influences the choices we make. No one wants to appear different in a world that screams at us daily to buy what will make us look good, and to socialise where it might be advantageous for career or status.

Young offender centres are populated with young people who got in with the 'wrong crowd'. Yes, they alone made the choice to sin, but what if their value system had been influenced differently? The pack mentality is strong, even for the more mature.

Let's take up the challenge to pray for and to set an example to the young people under our influence, to follow a Leader who will never lead them astray. One way we can do this is by following the advice given by Paul to the Roman believers when he said: "Don't copy the behaviour and customs of this world, but let God transform you into a new person by changing the way you think. Then you will learn to know God's will for you, which is good and pleasing and perfect" (Romans 12:2 NLT).

When we allow our thinking to be changed by God then we won't desire to follow the crowd. We'll be more interested in discovering God's good, pleasing, and perfect will for our lives.

Response

Judah did not always witness the best in his father and the family dynamic resulted in serious sibling rivalry. Then one day, far from home, the pack mentality overcame Jacob's sons and, led by Judah, they attacked Joseph. The choice Judah made that day started a domino effect of bad choices that he would eventually come to regret. He left home, married a Canaanite, and lived an immoral life that culminated in the incident with Tamar (Genesis 38). If it had not been for conscience – God's warning bell for the soul – Judah might never have responded correctly to the guilt that tormented him. Tamar called Judah out for his sin against her and it was the very thing that began a change in Jacob's fourth son (Genesis 38:25–26).

Judah had messed up big time, but God wasn't finished with him. As the Joseph story continues in the book of Genesis, we see Judah taking more of a leadership role than his brother Reuben. He is the one who convinces his father to allow them to return to Egypt for food and bring Simeon back home (Genesis 43). Later, Judah offers himself as a slave in place of Benjamin to avoid causing his father any further pain (Genesis 44:30–34). This is a picture of a changed man. Judah had reset his inner values and had determined to act righteously.

And his response produced a great reward. Not only were Judah, his father, and the whole family reunited and reconciled with Joseph, but God would use the descendants of Judah to instigate a kingly line that would ultimately produce Jesus, the Saviour of the world (Matthew 1).

Surely this is an encouragement for us to respond positively to our own feelings of guilt. The choices we make are vital to our future walk with God. Guilt robs us of a close relationship with God and stops us from serving with a pure heart. Peace can only be restored when we respond with genuine remorse to our God-given conscience.

- **Confession**: Confession of wrongdoing is an admission that what we have done has violated God's laws. But if we do not follow on to repentance then confession amounts to only mere words and cannot transform our hearts.

  Repentance involves much more. It requires not only an acknowledgment of our sin but a willingness to turn our back on it. It tells God that we are sorry for what we have done, that we don't want to repeat our mistakes and that we are prepared to change – or, more accurately, to *be* changed. Repentance is what unlocks the door to God's forgiveness which then restores our relationship with God.

  "I acknowledged my sin to you, and I did not cover my iniquity; I said: 'I will confess my transgressions to the LORD,' and you forgave the iniquity of my sin" (Psalm 32:5).

Every sin we commit is ultimately against God, and therefore it is to Him we should confess. When Nathan the prophet confronts King David concerning his adultery with Bathsheba and the death of her husband, Uriah (2 Samuel 11–12:24), David immediately confesses: "I have sinned against the Lord". Did he seduce Bathsheba? Yes (2 Samuel 11:4). Did he arrange for Uriah's death? Yes (2 Samuel 11:14). But David could not confess to Uriah – he was dead. Bathsheba had guilt of her own to deal with. Therefore, when faced with what he had done, David owned up. He knew his sin was against God. All of Psalm 51 is David's public confession and plea for forgiveness:

"For I know my transgressions, and my sin is ever before me.
Against you, and you only, have I sinned
and done evil in your sight…
Create in me a clean heart, O God,
and renew a right spirit within me."
Psalm 51:3–4, 10

What about those we have wronged?

Jesus tells us in Matthew 5:23–24 that if someone has something against you then you need to go them and be reconciled, so that it doesn't interfere with your worship. And James 5:16 says "confess your sins to each other" as it is important for your healing. This is the tough part. Pride will try to hold you back, and the person you have wronged may not forgive you, but it is incumbent on us to attempt to put things right where possible.

- **Commitment**: God is in the business of making all things new (2 Corinthians 5:17). He gives us new starts rather than second chances and expects us to live like we believe it. So, accept His forgiveness, ditch the guilt and commit to "love the Lord your God with all your heart and with all your soul and with all your mind" (Matthew 22:37).

It can be a frightening decision to follow Jesus in total commitment as it involves self-denial and sacrifice (Luke 9:23–24) and a value system to live by that is set by the Bible. A high standard indeed. Surely this kind of commitment sets us up for failure? Not so. Just as our salvation depends on what Christ accomplished for us on the cross (Isaiah 53:4–6) so the power to live as God expects comes through the power of the Holy Spirit now living within us. For it is "according to the riches of his glory he may *grant* you to be strengthened with power through his Spirit in your inner being" (Ephesians 3:16 emphasis mine). Remembering that our God "is able to do far more abundantly than all that we ask or think, according to the power at work within us" (Ephesians 3:20).

It's time to live differently (Ephesians 4:1). Let's imitate Christ (1 Corinthians 11:1)!

Guilt: Taking a closer look

For personal or group study

Study questions

1 Familiarise yourself with Judah's story as found in Genesis 37:18–36, 38, 42–45. Record where you think Judah went wrong.

2 Hatred is destructive. Consider Proverbs 10:12 and 1 John 2:9. How would Philippians 4:8 help us to avoid hatred?

3 Our society often says: "Don't get mad, get even" – but the Bible teaches us to respond differently. Examine Romans 12:17–21.

4 Is godly sorrow the same thing as guilt? Why/why not? Consider 2 Corinthians 7:10.

5 How can our conscience be cleansed? Hebrews 9:14 is a good place to start your investigation.

6 We are encouraged to help others struggling with situations from the past. How can Romans 15:1, Philippians 2:4 and Galatians 6:2, help us in this?

7 As you've read through Judah's story, has God pricked your conscience with something you thought was long buried? Perhaps now is a good time for confession (Proverbs 28:13), repentance (Romans 2:4), and recommitment (Galatians 2:20).

8 Remember you are loved. Whatever happened in the past cannot change God's love towards you. See for yourself in Jeremiah 31:3.

5

AGEING
SIMEON AND ANNA

I

c. 4 BC

"Mosheh!"

A groan emanated from beneath the blanket on the opposite side of the room, while the grey light of early morning tried to sneak through the cracks in the door. The sun had not fully risen from her sleep but someone else had. Mosheh turned on the straw pallet, eyes squeezed tight shut, a silent prayer for patience forming in his heart.

"Mosheh!"

The summons came again, louder this time.

"Mosheh! Where are my sandals?"

"Go to sleep, Father, the sun has not yet risen."

"Just because the sun has chosen to be lazy this morning does not mean I have to be. Now, where are my sandals?"

"Be quiet, Father, you'll waken Sarai."

"Have you hidden them again, Mosheh? Where are they? I need to get to the Temple."

By now the commotion of the search was louder than the words spoken, the clatter of a falling stool having wakened the one Mosheh hoped would stay asleep.

"Now look what you've done, Father!"

"Just give him his sandals, Mosheh," his wife grunted, "before he wakens up the whole street."

"Please go back to bed Father," Mosheh pleaded. "I don't like you going out so early. It's cold… and still dark."

"Mosheh!"

This time it was Sarai's reprimand that startled the ageing son.

"Mosheh," she repeated, "give your father his sandals. He won't listen to you. He's stubborn… and…"

"Sarai?" Mosheh turned towards his wife, "show some respect. Don't you know the Law?"

"Mosheh, if you don't give me my sandals I shall take yours! Then if I fall it will be your fault!"

Mosheh wearily pulled himself up from the mattress, convinced that the neighbours could hear his painful joints creak as he stood in the pre-dawn light. The floor seemed a long way down these days. Removing the lid from the old, cracked grain pot standing erect in the corner of the room, he reached deep inside to retrieve the sandals he'd hidden the previous night after his father had gone to sleep. What would it take to stop this good and kind man from the madness of spending all his waking hours in the Temple? As the years passed and frailty intensified, rather than pulling back, Mosheh's father had become more obsessed than ever with his quest.

He steadied the old man while he slipped his feet into the pieces of leather that had caused the early morning argument. By now Mosheh's hair was as grey as the father who had been the light of his life since ever he could remember. Hands wrapped around the old man's bony arms, Mosheh looked into his thinning face noticing a light that had never faded behind his clouded eyes. If anything, it seemed brighter than ever this morning.

"Father?"

"Don't worry about me, Mosheh," the old man said, gently tapping his son's cheek with twisted fingers. "Nothing can happen to me until the promise is fulfilled. I'll be fine."

"But you are unsteady..."

"I'll take my staff."

"It's cold..."

"I have my prayer shawl," he interjected, stretching for the woollen shawl as he reached the door. "You worry too much, Mosheh... it might be today."

"You say that every day, Father."

"Ah, but I have a feeling about today, Mosheh... I have a feeling."

As the door creaked shut Mosheh also had a feeling about today. It could be his father's last.

II

"Priests, arise and begin your duties! Levites, to your platform! Israelites, man your stations!"

Anna smiled. Her joints ached as the night slowly began its exit, yet every morning her heart warmed when she heard G'Vinay's wake-up call from the darkness of her tiny room. Another day would soon dawn. Another day closer to the fulfilment of the promise. Another day to worship while she waited for the consolation of Israel. Anna was grateful for another day.

"Will it be today, *Adonai*?" she whispered from her mattress, the sound of footsteps resonating through the darkness as priests made their way to the Chamber of Hewn Stone for the first lottery.

The old woman admired those who rose before the sun did, while night's cold blanket still lay heavy on the Temple's stone magnificence.

The keen and enthusiastic among Aaron's descendants never wanted to miss an opportunity to be involved in every aspect of the daily service. G'Vinay's bidding always provided a goodly number to draw from, even for what some might class as the more mundane of priestly duties.

Soon the glow of flaming torches flitted briefly under Anna's door as the dawn patrol passed by, checking every corner of the courts that would shortly fill with the faithful, the pilgrims, and the curious. For now, while the sun still slept beneath the eastern horizon, Anna basked in the privilege of dwelling in the courts of the Most High.

"How lovely is your dwelling place, O Lord of hosts!"

Turning on to her front, prostrated, her arms stretched out as though they would reach Heaven itself. Her lips moved, but Anna's early morning psalm of praise was silent enough not to disturb what was happening beyond her bedchamber.

"My heart and flesh sing for joy to the living God," she continued. "Blessed are those who dwell in your house, ever singing your praise!"

This offering of worship would reach God's throne before the cold ashes of yesterday's sacrifices had been removed from the altar.

"A day in your courts is better than a thousand elsewhere."

For many years, Anna had experienced the delight of living in the very courts she sang about. She saw laying her head each night on a straw-filled mattress, in a room void of any of life's comforts, as better than sleeping on the finest silk sheets of any palace. Nothing could compare with the knowledge that yards from her living quarters stood the Holy of Holies – the place where God met with man. To this godly woman, the courts she had access to filled with God's presence as much as the Holy Place where sacrifice was made on her behalf by the priests. God was in this place and Anna had no desire ever to leave it.

"I would rather be a doorkeeper in the house of my God than dwell in the tents of wickedness," she murmured.

Yet, as a woman, Anna couldn't be a doorkeeper in the Lord's house, but she had been granted what no other woman had ever enjoyed – to make her home in the Temple precincts.

"No good thing does He withhold from those…"

"Peace! All is peaceful!" broadcast the dawn patrol, their announcement briefly interrupting the old woman's repetition of the ancient song of pilgrimage.

"… who walk uprightly."

As is my soul at peace, Lord, but it continually yearns for your Sent-One. Will Messiah come soon? Our land is in such turmoil. Your people lie under the burden of sin, and Rome. Their affliction is great.

Anna breathed deeply as though the weight of these burdens required the deepest intake of air to meet her body's need. But she would not allow the external to stop her from completing her early morning psalm of praise.

"O Lord of hosts, blessed is the one who trusts in you."

It was the rumbling of her stomach that caused Anna to turn once again on the thin mattress. Hunger had become the tool she used to concentrate both mind and heart on God. It wasn't that she didn't have any food. The priests and the faithful often brought food to the old woman of the Temple, in recognition of her fervency and devotion. Yet few realised how often she gave that very same food away to others she saw as in greater need than herself, or that she fasted more often than the Law required. Anna's fasting was something between her and her God. Her face would never bear the ash of false humility that the Pharisees wore when they fasted. Unlike them, she didn't want to draw attention to herself, or seek the applause of others.

Anna fasted because she loved her Creator and sought His response on the issues that troubled her heart. It was as simple as that.

The noise around her increased as grey light began to replace the blackness of night in Jerusalem. Anna could identify every sound that emanated from beyond her room's small wooden door, most now originating from behind the Nicanor Gate – from the cranking of the wooden pulley that drew the huge copper laver from the water source below the place of sacrifice, to the calls shouted by the priests at various stages of the preparation for the daily sacrifice. Each sound was symbolic of an important step towards that which was required for the national and personal purging of sin.

At the age of eighty-four, Anna's bones felt the cold more keenly now. She wrapped the blanket more tightly around her. It was a gift from a beautiful teenager Anna had known since the girl's parents first brought her to the Temple as a newborn seeking God's blessing on their precious child. Anna had not been blessed with children, something that had grieved her down through the years. As she stroked the blanket against her cheek, it wasn't only childlessness that pulled at her heart. Even after all this time, the smiling face forming in her memory pulled her back decades to those vibrant days of her youth when the first sight to greet her each morning was the face of her darling husband. For seven short years, the only blemish on their perfect marriage was Anna's slowness to conceive, something her husband never chided her for. She was young, he was patient. Neither of them could never have imagined that time was not on their side.

Anna's mind often visited the day of her husband's death. She had learned that grief cannot be erased. It is merely managed. Yet after losing the love of her life, Anna only ever sought the presence of One other, and in doing so discovered the truth in the prophet Isaiah's words: "the reproach of your widowhood you will remember no more. For your Maker is your husband, the Lord of hosts is his name... For the Lord has called you like a wife deserted and grieved in spirit" (Isaiah 52:4–6).

A smile crossed her face as she pushed the sorrow down once more, thankful for this new Husband who now filled her days with purpose and the assurance of His eternal love.

"The time has arrived!" echoing through the Temple drew Anna back from her reverie, the call announcing that soon the gates of the sanctuary would be open to the public. She must ready herself for the day. As she reached for the jug and basin in the corner of the room, an unusual sense of excitement came from deep within.

"What is it, my Lord?" she asked. "Do you have someone special for me to meet today?"

III

The path to the Temple seemed steeper today than it did yesterday. Simeon leant against a wall to catch his breath, thankful that he had brought his stick.

"*Adonai*," he whispered, too breathless to speak any louder. "If You allow a man to live this long, You should at least give him the energy to do so more easily."

Simeon knew his Maker would catch the humour in his words. Wasn't it the Lord who once used a donkey to speak to a wayward prophet! They had certainly talked together enough over the years. No one knew the old man better. And it was doubtful that any man spoke with his Creator more than Simeon did… or listened more carefully for that matter.

The colour of the night sky above him was changing to resemble the silver of Simeon's own hair. Soon the heavens would turn to gold and Simeon wanted to be at the gates before that happened. If what he'd heard in the night was true, he didn't dare miss a minute in God's courts today. He needed to be there when the gates opened. He'd waited too long for this day. The very thought of which caused his heart to race and his palms to sweat.

"I'm on my way, *Adonai*, wait for me… please."

A sudden pain caught the old man as he stretched to continue his journey, the ache knocking him off balance and almost into the path of a passing market trader. Bringing his cart to an abrupt halt, the trader stretched out his arm to prevent the fall, steadying Simeon once more against the wall.

"Are you all right, Simeon?" the younger man asked, an anxious look crossing his weather-beaten face. "Would you like me to take you home?"

"No, no… thank you," Simeon replied, embarrassment shaking off the stranger's strong arm. "I'm heading for the Temple. I'm fine. I don't need your help."

The young man shrugged his broad shoulders, smiled at Simeon's stubborn independence, and reached for the handles of his cart.

"How do you know my name?" Simeon questioned, ashamed of his initial abrupt response to his rescuer.

"Everyone knows you, Simeon," the trader replied, a wry smile crossing his face. "Every son of Israel, that is. My mother told me of the day you peered into my newborn face at the Temple. She left sad when you remarked that 'I was not the One'."

Steadying his load, the rescuer nodded a goodbye: "And after all, those who visit the Temple know you, for it seems you have been there longer than many of the stones that hold it together.

"Good day to you, Simeon," he said, "and may the Messiah you wait for come before the Romans render it impossible."

"The Lord make His face to shine upon you," Simeon replied. "Do not give up hope. The Promised One is close at hand. *Adonai* will not fail us... not even the Romans can thwart God's plan."

The streets of the lower city were starting to come to life by the time Simeon was steady enough to continue his journey. Traders were already calling the faithful to stop with them for items they deemed essential for their worship, the gullible too swift to part with their money. Urgency energised the old man's stiff limbs as the horizon brightened and the crowds thickened. The sight of the Temple watchman already in position unsettled Simeon, but it was the first call of Dawn that caused him to doubt he'd reach the gates in time.

"BARKAI!" shouted the watchman. "The day has dawned!"

Do they know, Adonai? Do they know that this is the day?

The reply to Simeon's silent question came from a place the old man usually managed to keep in check. Not so on this occasion as doubt answered, *how many times have you asked that question, old man?*

"The entire eastern horizon is illuminated," yelled the watchman, his words thankfully restoring Simeon's equilibrium.

Simeon pushed forward, causing some consternation among the gathered crowd of mostly traders. The rush for the morning sacrifice would not come until a little later – the very crowd Simeon did not want to miss.

"Does the dawn extend all the way to Hebron?" questioned a lone voice from behind the gates.

"Yes!" came the reply, signalling permission to the Levites below to open the gates to the Sanctuary.

He'd made it! Breathless, exhausted, and feeling every one of his many years, yet satisfied in heart that he was in his place for the event God had told him about all those years ago. Though at times he had grown impatient, never once had he doubted what was now embedded in his heart. God had promised Simeon that he would not die until he had seen the Son of Consolation – the long-awaited Messiah – with his own eyes. As he walked the space between the outside world and the Temple complex, Simeon became deeply aware of the Holy Spirit's presence. Such was the enormity of that presence that the old man dropped to his knees in awe and worship. The grandeur around him, displayed in marble and gold, could not equate with the Presence now within.

He'd already heard the sacrificial lamb being called for. Knew that in a few short hours he would join with the men and priests of Israel to watch that sacrifice for their sin burn on the grand altar. Afterwards, he would stretch prostrate in silence as the service of incense rose heavenward to bless God Himself, inhaling a fragrance sweeter than any other on earth. And his ears would hear the Levite choir sing a psalm before the Aaronic blessing was conferred on all present.

Yet none of it could compare with what he was about to witness. God on earth in human form – the Hope of Israel – come to rescue, comfort, and deliver His people. The prophecies of centuries were about to be fulfilled and he, Simeon, would be given the gift to recognise the God-child who would make it happen.

All those years of rushing at each newborn, trying to use his own wisdom to recognise the Sent-One. The many times a mother had looked into his eyes longing that the old man of the Temple would declare her son as Messiah. The multitude of evenings he had walked the crowded streets home, deflated and disappointed yet again. Praying every new day that would be the day the promise would be fulfilled. And when sickness touched his human frame he would plead that God would spare him until the day he would see Messiah for himself.

Yet, on that day when God spoke to Simeon's listening heart, promising his younger self that he would meet the Promised One in the flesh, he hadn't realised that all God was ever asking him to do was wait. The same Spirit that had revealed God's promise would tell him when the time was right. However, impatience seemed to be encoded into the human psyche and Simeon had spent his years not only waiting for, but physically looking for, the Consolation of Israel. Occasionally the butt of jokes, and even the subject of gossip, Simeon was unaffected by how he was seen and spoken about. Nothing else mattered, God had spoken.

Taking his position in the shade of the colonnades, the old man felt his heart pounding against his ribs. Yet strangely, alongside the excitement, a sense of peace flowed over him with the freshness of the spring waters cascading the slopes of Mount Hermon.

Lifting silent praise to the covenant-keeping God, Simeon vowed that today he would not search out the families visiting the Temple for the sacrifice of purification. Instead, he would save his gaze for the One he had been sent to meet. This time he would wait… wait for the Spirit to direct his feet… and oh, Simeon was ready.

IV

Anna always waited until she heard the sanctuary gates open before she left her sleeping quarters. The privilege afforded to her of lodging in the Temple complex was something she never wanted to lose. So, she kept closely to the rules, careful to avoid crossing any boundaries that might be seen as a step too far, especially by the Pharisees. Apart from the priests who had travelled from all over Israel to complete their required service, there were a few others who stayed occasionally at the Temple, mainly the Levites who were involved in cleaning duties.

Yet, many of the religious leaders looked on housing a woman on Temple grounds as sacrilege at worst, or disrespectful at best... even a woman of Anna's age. Yet none of them could get past the obvious spirituality of the daughter of Phanuel, from the tribe of Asher. Some even dared to call her a prophetess, a title Anna disliked.

Listening, however, was something Anna did relish, a skill she had developed over her years of public service. Daily she watched the broken, widowed, hungry, desolate, and lonely walk these courts she called home. She'd learned to weep with those who wept, and to rejoice with those who had come with full hearts to offer thanks to God for His blessing. And in the mix of the multitude, she prayed for God to guide her to those who needed a listening ear, a compassionate heart, and perhaps even a word from the Lord if He so directed her.

However, it was a different kind of listening that caused others to view Anna as special. The kind of listening that allowed Anna to hear God speak – whether it was through the writings of the Torah or the words of the prophets that she heard from the edge of the crowds gathered around the rabbis. Or the silent listening for God's voice she had cultivated in her spirit, whether in the crowds, or more often than not, in the stillness of her room after the Temple gates had slammed shut for the night. In noise or silence, Anna listened for the only voice which always spoke truth, wisdom, knowledge, and hope to her heart.

"Lord, Your prophet Amos said: 'For the Lord God does nothing without revealing his secret to his servants the prophets,'" Anna whispered, as the sound of passing traders broke into her prayers.

"Speak, Lord, I am Your devoted servant."

The air around her moved as though another was in the room. But she didn't need to look for some stranger, the old woman knew her Guest well. His felt presence was no longer uncommon. Such was the other-worldly feeling of such visits that she often wondered if this was what the High Priest experienced in the Holy of Holies on the annual Day of Atonement, when he sprinkled the sacrificial blood on the Mercy Seat of the Ark, to atone for the sins of the nation.

For years she'd tried to imagine what it must be like to be so close to the symbol of God's presence on earth? The very thought of it had kept her awake at night, excited her, sometimes frightened her. Often she had lamented being born a woman, and of Asher's tribe of bakers rather than Aaron's tribe of priests. Entering the Holy of Holies could never be for the likes of her.

But Anna had discovered that God does not hide behind walls of marble or gates of gold. She almost laughed with delight the first time she heard the words of Jeremiah echo beneath the colonnades: "You will seek me and find me," says the Lord, "when you seek me with all your heart." *God wants me to seek Him! He can be found!*

Now, years later, sitting in the *found* presence, Anna bowed low, reverence and worship as natural to her as breathing. Even as an old woman, she lived daily in God's promise – a promise given to His people down through their history – that He would never forsake them. That He would always be with them.

The longer she worshipped, the more fervently she prayed, the more obvious was God's presence in her life. There were even times, like now, that the God of Heaven sat beside her in her little room while the world outside rushed by.

"What is it, Master?" Anna questioned. "Is He near?"

The question was not new, but this time she was prompted to extend it. "Is He here?"

V

Simeon jerked! Shaking himself for the second time in the same number of minutes the old man struggled to stay awake. An interrupted night's sleep, combined with his early rise and near accident did nothing to encourage his heavy eyelids to remain open.

"*Adonai*," he said, a little too loudly to avoid the stares of a few passers-by. Adjusting the volume of his petition, Simeon continued.

"*Adonai*, my spirit is willing, but my ancient body is declaring its need for sleep." Frustration deepened the lines crossing his forehead. "Send your angels to hold my eyelids up, or I shall miss the fulfilment of Your promise."

"Simeon," called a voice that the old man knew was not God's. "Are you feeling ill?" Simeon glanced upwards. "You seem perturbed. Can I help?" the stranger continued.

"Why does everyone think I need assistance today?" he snorted, "I am perfectly fine. I am simply waiting for the Consolation of Israel."

"Aren't we all, dear friend... aren't we all?"

As the young man turned to go, Simeon called to him, "Apologies, Young Sir. I would be grateful for your help. Perhaps you could take my elbow and help this old fool towards the Nicanor Gate. It sounds as if the sacrifice is about to begin."

The two walked across the Court of Women, joining the men making their way to the Court of Israel for the daily sacrifice. Simeon wasn't the only one needing help. Others also steadied their elders as they mounted the steep steps, adding safety from the jostling crowd. As Simeon lifted his head, the tall towers of the Antonia Fortress created an unwelcome sight, reminding the worshippers that they were an occupied nation, always watched by their oppressors, even in worship. Sadness touched Simeon's heart. Yet, just as quickly it lifted again as a thought struck the old man.

Aha! No matter how closely the Romans spy on us, they will never recognise the One I will meet today!

A chuckle left his lips, and the young man at his elbow felt Simeon's step suddenly lighten, and with it a "presence" such as he had never experienced before. *Was this what God's presence felt like?* he wondered, his own heart now racing. Such was his excitement, that he didn't want to let go of this man who was connecting him more with God than anything else had within these courts.

The loud clatter of the Magrepha thrown from the altar's ramp to the ground signalled the service was about to begin, and as the Levite choir took their places, Simeon and his young helper prostrated themselves alongside the faithful.

From her quarters Anna had also heard the rake fall.

Today, rather than scrambling with the other women for a place on the verandas to attempt a glimpse of the proceedings, she chose to worship in the quietness of her room. She knew that, once outside, the noise of the everyday would crowd out the wonder of God's presence she was experiencing at that very moment. Instead, her head remained bowed low, her forehead touching the thin woven mat on the ground as the smell of incense crept below her door.

"The Lord bless you and keep you," she recited, barely able to hear the priests recite the Aaronic blessing from that distance. "The Lord make his face to shine upon you and be gracious to you," her words joining with theirs. "The Lord lift up his countenance upon you and give you peace."

A few minutes passed while Anna thought on the offerings of the lamb, meal, and wine now being offered on the great altar. She was only too aware of her own need of forgiveness as well as that of her nation. Thankful that God had made a way for this to happen, if only on a temporary basis. The cymbals clashed, and the sound of the Levite choir rushed to fill every corner of the Temple complex, invariably flowing over the walls to the streets of the city beneath.

Three short blasts marked the end of the first stanza of Psalm 82. She had been in the Temple so long that she knew which psalm would be sung on which day. No, more than that, she knew each psalm by heart, for weren't they the very words God had ordered to be spoken. As the years rolled by each word had become sweeter to her than honey, just as the psalmist had said, and more desired than gold or anything money could buy.

Yet, as the years of her life had multiplied there was something Anna treasured even more – something which daily burned in her heart. God's promise of a Messiah – the One who would bring consolation – hope – to this weary nation. During the previous four hundred years of God's silence, many of her countrymen had doubted that a rescuer would ever come. Then, when it seemed that things couldn't get any worse, the Romans invaded! She was just a little girl when what looked to her like all the army of Rome trampled through Galilee on their way to Jerusalem, wreaking havoc, killing or arresting any who dared to get in the way. Even now she shuddered at the thought of General Pompey's desecration of the Holy of Holies.

Anna jumped at the third blast of the Shofar, chiding herself for allowing her thoughts to distract her from worship. *Thank you, Adonai, for understanding my shortcomings.*

The noise outside Anna's door had changed from reverential worship to the buzz of men dashing back to work, and Temple traders vociferously vying for customers. How quickly lives move on to the next thing, Anna thought, rising to her feet, brushing the creases from her dress as she did so.

"Anna."

She stopped, thinking she'd heard her name.

"Anna."

There it was again.

"Anna, it's time."

VI

"Can I help you return home, Simeon?" the young man asked, having safely returned the old man to the flat ground of the Court of Women.

"No, thank you," Simeon replied, a smile crossing his face. "I have important business to do here today."

"If you are sure," the young man responded, rather sad that he now had no excuse to stay with him for longer.

"You have been very kind, but I must be about my business. God be with you."

Simeon appeared anxious, impatient, or what? His helper couldn't quite figure out what was going on, apart from the fact that he was being dismissed. He tilted his head in a respectful nod, voicing his farewell. He was glad he had come to the Temple today, if only to have been in the presence of this old man he had heard so much about. When he walked away he couldn't resist glancing back, wondering what 'business' the old man had to transact? And in looking, he saw Simeon make his way towards a couple with a baby.

The usual greeting went unsaid as Simeon reached the young family coming away from a trader, two young pigeons now held firmly in the man's hands. Simeon's eyes went straight to the baby – forty days old no doubt, the pigeons indicating that their attendance at the Temple was for the mother's purification rites. But initially Simeon wasn't interested in the middle-aged man with the young wife. His attention was focused exclusively on the tiny boy in the young woman's arms.

So engrossed was he that he didn't notice the glances of those passing by. Some of the looks were pitiful in nature. Was Simeon up to his old tricks again? Others wondered if perhaps the old man of the Temple knew something they didn't.

However, the couple didn't seem at all perturbed by the elder's interruption on what was a very important day for them, presenting both mother and firstborn son at the Temple. It almost seemed as if they had had previous experience of strange intrusion into their lives.

Simeon's hands trembled. He stared deeply into the baby's dark brown eyes, bright with the charm of infancy that instantly stole the old man's heart. The baby caught Simeon's finger as he reached out to stroke his face, the little one wrapping his small hand tightly around it, as if he'd never let it go. The old man chuckled and the baby smiled. Oh, how long he had waited to see this smile. And with the faintest of glances towards the parents, Simeon lifted the baby out of his mother's arms and nestled him against his own heart.

The old man was overjoyed. Tears ran down the creases of his aged cheeks, but his spine seemed to straighten and muscles strengthen as he held the young child in his arms. And he blessed God for this moment, surprising even the baby's parents with his words.

"Sovereign Lord," Simeon's eyes lifted from the baby in his arms to the sky above, "now it is time for me to die in peace."

The baby's mother Mary looked at her husband Joseph with questioning eyes.

"For now I have seen Your salvation with my own eyes, just as You promised," the old man continued. "The salvation, declared through the prophets of old, that would come to all people is now here." And Simeon's eyes shifted back to contemplate the wriggling bundle he held. "Yes, Lord, *this* salvation will bring light to even the Gentiles and honour to Your people Israel, who gave Him life."

Meanwhile, through the crowd, Anna's eyes fell on the sight. Clutching her chest, she gasped, the air thick with delight and expectation, desire propelling her feet towards her friend Simeon and the young family.

He is here, Adonai, just as you said!

Mary and Joseph could hardly believe what they were hearing, surprise written over their faces, as Simeon's blessing changed from blessing God to blessing them. As he placed the baby back into his mother's arms, the old man's bony hands rested on each of the parents' heads.

"Listen carefully," he said, "this child will be the ruination of many in this land, bringing down the proud and arrogant, but... He will also exalt others beyond what could be imagined."

Anna arrived just as Simeon was finishing, daring not to interrupt as her dear friend prophesied over the child.

"The Lord God has appointed Him to reveal the hearts of men." Simeon paused looking compassionately into the young mother's eyes. "This will cause many to oppose Him… and… lead, one day, to your own heart being broken as surely as if a sword had pierced it."

Mary clung tightly to the little one as Simeon stepped back. Neither she, nor Joseph, could respond, each lost in their own thoughts – yet each remembering what the Angel had said eleven months earlier. And Mary added Simeon's words to the treasure that she had already begun storing in her heart. One thing was certain, theirs was no ordinary child. Only God could help them raise this little boy. Only God could prepare Him, and them, for whatever lay ahead.

Suddenly Simeon's grim pronouncement was turned upside down as an old woman started jumping up and down for joy, praising God for their son. Anna's exuberance spilled over to those around, who wondered what the old woman of the Temple was so excited about.

Mary and Joseph smiled, recognising that sorrow might lie ahead but knowing that, for now, they were here to give thanks to God for the safe arrival of their firstborn. Remarkably, the two young pigeons were still in Joseph's hands as they thanked Simeon and Anna for their blessings and set off to find the priest responsible for the personal sacrifices that would be offered that day.

Anna could hardly contain herself as she and Simeon rejoiced in the fulfilment of God's promise. Messiah was still a baby, but one day He would rise and rescue Israel. And these wise old saints somehow knew that peace wouldn't come through war or politics, for the real battle was not over territory or power. It was far more serious than that.

"Simeon?" Anna asked, before rushing off to tell her friends the wonderful news, "don't you wish you had another thirty years to see the end of the story?"

Simeon shrugged, a wide smile stretching his face at the thought.

"No, Anna," he replied. "I am at peace. I have seen all that God has planned for me. The Almighty is no doubt preparing others for the next part of His story."

The two parted in peace… perhaps for the last time.

Adapted from the story of Simeon and Anna found in Luke 2:22–40.

Ageing: Life lessons

The struggle

Just to clarify, Simeon and Anna were not related in any way.

However, their stories came together quite beautifully when Mary and Joseph attended the Temple forty days after Jesus' birth. The young couple had come to offer the required sacrifice for Mary's postnatal purification rites (Leviticus 12:3–4) and to present their firstborn son to the Lord.

Simeon and Anna undoubtedly knew each other by virtue of how often they were in the Temple, a practice that had spanned many years. It is also recognised both biblically and historically that they were members of a group of people whom the Bible refers to as "waiting for the consolation of Israel" (Luke 2:25, 38). This group was known by some as 'the quiet in the land'. They wanted Israel to be liberated just as much as did the vocal, and frequently violent, zealots, but they believed in a spiritual solution instead of a revolutionary one. Their method was found in devotion and worship. They believed intently that God would rescue Israel by sending a Messiah, in fulfilment of the many prophecies given to God's people down through many years (for example, Isaiah 7:14, 42:1-3).

The struggles of Simeon and Anna are different to the others we have considered in this book. Their inclusion is not because of something they did wrong, or because they had been wronged by others. And while not all of us can identify with the struggle of feeling trapped, spoiled, guilty, or a failure, every single one of us will eventually identify with Simeon and Anna. Unless God calls us Heavenward early in life, none of us can escape the challenges of ageing, which might also include a conviction that our days of usefulness in God's kingdom are behind us.

Simeon and Anna show us that nothing could be further from the truth – no matter how old we are, God isn't finished with us yet.

Unlike Anna, we are not told Simeon's age. However, because of the respect the Gospel writer afforded Simeon, along with the opening words of what has become known as the *Nunc Dimittis*, it is believed Simeon had indeed reached a great age. In fact, his encounter with the infant Jesus drew a rather unexpected response from him. "Sovereign Lord," he said, "now let your servant die in peace, as you have promised" (Luke 2:29 NLT). Such a reaction would not have been expected from a younger man. It appears that Simeon was feeling his age and having been given the supreme privilege of identifying the Lord's Christ, he was ready to leave life behind. He believed his life's work was over as the word of prophecy given to him (Luke 2:26) had now been fulfilled.

We are told Anna's age, although even this has raised minor controversary. Was she eighty-four years old, or was it eighty-four years since her husband died (Luke 2:36–37)? It is not hugely important as the text clearly states, "she was advanced in years" (verse 36), although the latter assumption would make her over one hundred years old!

Today, certainly in Western culture, it is perceived that accomplishments in life are the domain of the young. It would be foolish not to agree with this in certain circumstances, but then not everything of importance, whether secular or spiritual, requires an agile body nor a quick mind. God makes it clear that He is more interested in how we are on the inside than on our physical prowess (1 Samuel 16:7).

The struggle Simeon and Anna undoubtedly experienced came in the form of the physical restraints and ailments of an ageing body. Mother Nature is not kind where ageing is concerned, particularly in the area of memory and especially in diseases of the brain now known as dementia, in its various forms. Perhaps Simeon and Anna might also have struggled with waiting... waiting for God to answer their prayers... waiting for God to fulfil His promises. Waiting, year after year, and hearing nothing but silence. Sitting in God's waiting room is not fun at any time of life, and even less so as the years progress.

Yet the Bible has much to say about growing old and is quick to give us examples of those who, in their later years, were greatly used by God.

- **Noah** was four hundred and eighty years old when God told him to build the ark (Genesis 6:14–18). True, people lived much longer pre-flood, but Noah was not a young man when he started his building project, and he was one hundred and twenty years older when he finished.
- **Abraham** was seventy-five when he first heard God's call to leave his idol worship and everything that was familiar to him. "Go from your country," the unknown God said to him, "and your kindred and your father's house to the land that I will show you" (Genesis 12:1). God didn't even tell this particular old man where He was taking him.

- **Moses** was an eighty-year-old shepherd in the back of beyond when God told him to return to Egypt, where he was a wanted man. The reason? To rescue a nation from slavery (Exodus 3:1–12).
- **Caleb** was eighty-five years old when he left the wilderness after the Egyptian exodus, and it was said of him that he was as strong for battle then as when he was aged forty-five (Joshua 14:11).
- **Isaiah** prophesied fifty-five to sixty years through the reigns of three kings to bring the wayward nation of Judah back to God. But his greatest role in life was to prophesy concerning the coming Messiah, the accuracy of which astounds readers even in our day (see Isaiah 52:13 – 53:12,).
- **Apostle John** outlived all the other disciples, leaving us the Gospel of John; his letters of first, second, and third John; as well as the book of Revelation. Remarkably, he wrote Revelation from the prison mines on the Isle of Patmos when he was around ninety-nine years old.

And that's only a few, without even mentioning Anna and Simeon whom we are currently discussing.

My usual response when I read the stories of people like those listed is to think they must have been remarkably gifted individuals, and therefore nothing like me. But nothing could be further from the truth. Each one was an ordinary human being – just like me – but they had an unshakeable belief in the power of God, along with a deep desire to worship Him through self-sacrifice and obedience. Yet, their ordinariness also included mistakes. They were far from perfect, but then God tells us, "My grace is sufficient for you, for my power is made perfect in weakness" (2 Corinthians 12:9). Perhaps it's when the confidence of youth passes that we become more willing for God's strength rather than our ability to come to the fore.

Reputation

Reputation is not something that happens overnight. It is the generally held opinion or belief about someone that has been gained over time. A person's reputation concerning their work, trust, or character, is built up gradually until it becomes commonly accepted. Unfortunately, a bad reputation can be even more memorable than a good one, but harder to lose.

Over many years, Simeon had gained a reputation summarised in just two words, "righteous" and "devout" (Luke 2:25). It said a lot about the man to whom God chose to introduce His Son – the Messiah.

To be seen as righteous is to do with how we treat others, and how we conduct ourselves in the public arena. It speaks to our relationships in business, friendships, and with family. Can we be trusted? Are we people of integrity? Do we always speak truthfully? Do we treat everyone the same, whatever their station in life? It certainly appears that Simeon was such a man, for the writer felt it was important to describe his reputation.

How we conduct ourselves, whether with individuals, in employment, or even in church is our responsibility, as Proverbs 20:11 says, "Even a child makes himself known by his acts, by whether his conduct is pure and upright."

But the interpretation of our character and actions by others is not always accurate, is it? Many a reputation has run aground on the rocks of false perception, or defamation cast by someone with an ulterior motive than our good. Rumour and innuendo are as destructive as fire, but the writer of the book of Proverbs makes an excellent point: "Without wood a fire goes out; without a gossip a quarrel dies down" (Proverbs 26:20 NIV). Let's make sure we don't add wood to a fire that should never have been lit, for one day it could be our reputation that goes up in smoke. Titus reminds us to "speak evil of no one, to avoid quarrelling, to be gentle, and to show perfect courtesy toward all people" (Titus 3:2).

My dad left school aged fourteen and worked in labouring jobs all his life. He was deeply respected by all who knew him, building up a reputation that impressed the boss in exactly the same way as it did the teaboy. His secret wasn't only in his work ethic... he was a Titus 3:2 man, he "showed perfect courtesy toward all people". Something he tried to instil in his children.

During my nurse training, I was due to move to a ward where the sister had the reputation as a battleaxe. I was terrified of her before I'd even met her! My dad's advice settled my heart, "Don't listen to rumours, Catherine. Form your own opinions of people. Fill in the blank sheet you have of this woman with your own words, not those of others. Give her the same chance you'd like her to give you."

Such wisdom.

But what can we do if our reputation has been unfairly trashed?

- **Remember Jesus words:** "In the world you will have tribulation. But take heart; I have overcome the world" (John 16:33). An easy ride isn't promised to any of us in this life, especially if we belong to Jesus. The enemy of our souls will seek any way possible to trip us up, often through the foolish talk of others, and even blatant lies. But Jesus encourages us to remember that He is ultimately in control, even if we experience temporary setbacks.
- **Choose your reaction carefully:** The natural reaction is to retaliate, but sometimes saying nothing is more powerful. However, if setting the record straight is required, then it's best done face to face. The constant to-and-froing of today's digital communications can be the cause of many interpersonal difficulties. You cannot always read the intent behind words typed in haste and read on a small screen. Talk things over, and if no progress is made then follow the advice of Matthew 18:15–17 to set things straight. In every circumstance, "Let your speech always be gracious, seasoned with salt, so that you will know how you ought to answer each person" (Colossians 4:6). Or you might just manage to lose your reputation all by yourself.
- **Decide to be better not bitter:** The actions of others can indeed cause devastation, so ask God what He wants you to learn from it. Pray for those opposed to you that they will recognise their sin and put things right. Pray for yourself "that no 'root of bitterness' springs up and causes trouble" (Hebrews 12:15).
- **Factor in the big picture:** Life isn't all about me, but God can and does work together all things for the good of those who love Him (Romans 8:28). God wants us to trust Him, even when we can't see how any good can come from our predicament.
- **Prioritise your identity in Christ:** Focus on what is truly important – your salvation and your place in God's family. Allow Him to vindicate you in His time, and "Trust in the Lord with all your heart, and do not lean on your own understanding. In all your ways acknowledge him, and he will make straight your paths" (Proverbs 3:5–6).
- Relax… He's got your back!

I'm sure Simeon's reputation had taken a knock down through the years. After all, he'd made known God's promise to reveal the Messiah to him personally, before he died. As the years passed without sign of the Promised One, I have no doubt the old man had criticism and perhaps even mockery flung his way, but Simeon's faith did not waver. It was God's reputation that was on the line. All Simeon had to do was believe. That obviously came easy to him as Luke described him not only as "righteous" but "devout" (Luke 2:25).

While being righteous spoke of Simeon's relationships with others, being devout tells us of Simeon's relationship with God. And while the word 'devout' is not used of Anna, her way of life was a window into what the word means. She loved God's house to such an extent that she didn't want to leave it, while her love for God was displayed in frequent self-denial (Luke 2:37). Her days were filled with worship, her nights were filled with prayer, and she loved to fellowship with others who felt the same way as she did (Luke 2:38). You could not look at Anna and miss the driving force of her life.

These two also knew the meaning of true worship. It was a lifestyle, not an add-on to their week. God was at the centre of their lives. Everything else was secondary. Their focus in life was to wait for the One to whom the Old Testament Scriptures pointed. They not only believed in the redemption and rescue of Israel, but they also knew the Messiah was the only source of hope for Israel and for their own difficult lives. The promise of His coming was as real to them as His presence should be to us today.

This was the testimony they bore to Jesus... before they'd even met Him!

What kind of a reputation do we want to follow, or to proceed, us? Can it be said that we are "righteous" in our dealings with others? Is our devotion to the One who gave His all for our redemption (Isaiah 53:5) clearly visible in our daily lives, and not only on a Sunday? Do we worship God in "spirit and in truth" (John 4:24)? Where does self-denial fit into my spiritual walk?

Simeon and Anna are wonderful examples on how God's children should live their lives and have their focus. Paul continues that challenge with his words to the young believers in Thessalonica recorded in 1 Thessalonians.

"Our purpose is to please God, not people. He alone examines the motives of our hearts."
(1 Thessalonians 2:4 NLT)

Patience

"Practice makes perfect" is a well-proven saying, certainly as true in the spiritual realm as in the physical.

While some of us are gifted in certain areas, requiring less practice before we reach the required standard, others among us need to try again and again… and again… before we get it right.

Patience is a point in question.

Patience – the capacity to tolerate delay – is a test few of us master without major effort. Whether it's the simple everyday annoyances or situations that we believe require urgent action. It's one area of life where we need plenty of practice to get it perfect.

God, however, needs no practice in the patience stakes. It's an unchangeable part of the divine nature.

Paul puts it plainly: "Don't you see how wonderfully kind, tolerant and patient God is with you?" (Romans 2:4 NLT). While Peter explains that God's patience is nothing to do with being slow, but rather because of His great love for us. "The Lord is not slow to fulfil his promise as some count slowness, but is patient toward you, not wishing that any should perish, but that all should reach repentance" (2 Peter 3:9).

The great wordsmith Max Lucado describes it beautifully: "Patience is the red carpet upon which God's grace approaches us!"[7] Such grace goes beyond salvation from sin to what God knows we need in every area of our lives, often flipping the patience coin to where He asks us to be the patient ones. There are things God asks us to wait for. He teaches us patience in the waiting – not merely a resigned tolerance – but rather, an acceptance void of annoyance and anxiety. Patience is built on a foundation of trust in the One who knows our prayers, desires, and painful circumstances. We say, "We need You to do something now, Lord." God replies, often through silence, "I need you to trust Me… and wait." Trusting and waiting are the bedfellows of patience.

Our lives are ruled by the impatient tick-tock of time, while God, from the standpoint of eternity, never seems to be in a hurry – something we clock-watchers find frustrating.

Ageing eventually changes the speed of life's clock, slowing body and mind to differing degrees. We can't do things with the same speed we used to, but then neither is our day filled with the same number of tasks that require our attention. Yet, as the years pass, our foundation of trust has been added to so many times that patience stands securely on it. The more acquainted we become with God, the easier it is to believe that "His way is perfect" (Psalm 18:30), and that "The LORD is good to those who wait for Him" (Lamentations 3:25).

Patience is not a gift.

Paul names it as part of the fruit of the Spirit (Galatians 5:22–23). It's something that is grown in us by the Spirit's empowering. What little I do know about gardening is that growing something doesn't happen overnight. It takes time: the fruit of patience being an excellent example. In the waiting for God to answer our prayers, fulfil His promises, or give us the guidance we need, He grows in us the ability to trust Him without constant whining or fretting. Soon, those seeds of patience begin to swell. Faith takes root, reminding us that God is working for our good and for His kingdom. Each time our Heavenly Father keeps us waiting, the patience fruit becomes stronger, grows larger, and requires less cultivation than previously. Eventually, it becomes our go-to response when we pray. God shows us the waiting is worth it, no matter how difficult, "for it is God who works in you, both to will and to work for his good pleasure" (Philippians 2:13).

We are not told how long it was since "it had been revealed to him by the Holy Spirit that he would not see death before he had seen the Lord's Christ" (Luke 2:26), but clearly Simeon believed what he had been told. He continued to trust God's promise, and patiently waited for its fulfilment. I doubt that time alone produced patience in this old man, for Simeon was not the only one who waited for God to rescue Israel. It was a national pastime. But while the masses waited for a military general, Simeon, Anna and others (Luke 2:38) searched the ancient Scriptures for the signs of the coming Messiah. Yet even in this, Simeon's situation was altogether different.

Thirty-three years prior to Pentecost, we are told that Simeon's waiting was enabled and directed by the indwelling presence of the Holy Spirit (Luke 2:25ff). He had not only received a special revelation that Messiah would come in his lifetime, but direction from the Holy Spirit to go to the Temple on the very day Mary and Joseph were bringing Jesus to the Temple (Luke 2:27). By this time Simeon was well practised in patience, enabling him to experience the Spirit's prompting. Then, when the time came, Simeon was in his place, and the wait was worth it.

Hope

Hope was in short supply in Israel on the day Simeon and Anna met with Jesus.

They lived in occupied territory, ruled by a powerful force that had quite literally conquered the known world. Local government was appointed by Rome, with officials exacting exorbitant taxes to line their own pockets on top of meeting Rome's demands. Religious life had become tainted with additional laws (Matthew 23:4) weighing heavily on an already oppressed people. Poverty, with its resulting deprivation, ravaged the inhabitants like a plague. To make matters worse, the zealots' underground efforts against the Romans were as ineffective as a swarm of stingless bees. Added to all of this God was apparently unresponsive to His people's calls for help. All hope was gone. Or so it seemed.

Anna believed otherwise.

God was not silent. He spoke to her through the beauty around her, the daily readings in the Temple, the smell of the incense, the singing of the choir, and the smiles and tears of those she met every day. She recognised God's concern for His people everywhere. That concern filled her with hope in the faithful God who had proved to her over many years that He would make good on His promises (Deuteronomy 7:9). Anna had no doubt that those promises included sending help to His weary people. Hadn't her own father told her as a girl about Moses' final blessing on their tribe before they entered the Promised Land? "As your days, so shall your strength be" (Deuteronomy 33:25), Israel's deliverer had told them. Years later as a grown woman, after the untimely death of her husband, hadn't she proven the truth in those very words? God had given her the strength to get through even the worst of days.

Hope for Anna had to do with neither human desire, nor wishful thinking. Rather her desire for good in the future relied on God's power, not on her ability to muster enough energy to make it through such devastating loss. As the days merged into weeks, months, years, and eventually decades, this special widow had become deeply acquainted with the One she would have called *Adonai*. She had proved His faithfulness, which had transformed hope into certainty. Anna's future was as secure as God had proved her past to be.

The Old Testament Hebrew word for 'hope' translates into 'a cord' or 'an attachment', signifying safety through the attachment. The writer to the Hebrews expands that thought by calling out faith – our confidence in God – as the attachment which makes hope a certainty. "Faith shows the reality of what we hope for; it is the evidence of things we cannot see" (Hebrews 11:1 NLT).

Faith is trusting God now while, as John Piper says: "Hope is faith in the future tense. No uncertainty... instead a confident expectation and desire for something good in the future."[8]

Anna and Simeon didn't merely hope in some wishy-washy way that God would rescue Israel by sending the Messiah, they were certain of it. No ifs, no buts, no maybes. All the evidence they needed that God would come through on His word was based on many years of experiencing His faithfulness. God could be trusted. It was as simple as that.

And then one day they got to look into the face of Jesus!

Human hope seeks a good outcome, which may or may not happen. It carries no certainty. Christian hope looks back at what Christ has done for us, enabling us to leave our future with Him in time and for eternity.

The powerful words of Edward Mote (1834) capture the sentiment perfectly:

"My hope is built on nothing less
Than Jesus' blood and righteousness;
I dare not trust the sweetest frame,
But wholly lean on Jesus' name.

When darkness veils His lovely face
I rest on His unchanging grace;
In every high and stormy gale,
My anchor holds within the veil.

His oath, His covenant, His blood
Support me in the whelming flood;
When all around my soul gives way,
He then is all my hope and stay.

When He shall come with trumpet sound,
Oh, may I then in Him be found;
Dressed in His righteousness alone,
Faultless to stand before the throne.

On Christ, the solid Rock, I stand;
All other ground is sinking sand,
All other ground is sinking sand."[9]

When I was both young in years and in faith, I questioned too much. I struggled with life's pain, and even occasionally doubted God's love for me. I'm not proud of that, but the older I became, and the longer I stood on "Christ, the solid Rock" I discovered God's grace in the darkness and His anchor in the storm. When I felt I was drowning, and everything around me was disintegrating, Jesus alone became my hope, my security. And one day, when my life is over, I shall stand before Him faultless, clothed in His righteous robes... knowing full well that "this hope will not lead to disappointment. For we know how dearly God loves us, because he has given us the Holy Spirit to fill our hearts with his love" (Romans 5:5 NLT).

Ageing may have many disadvantages, but it gives us plenty of time and opportunity to learn in the school of faith. After all, as Job tells us: "Wisdom is with the aged, and understanding in length of days" (Job 12:12).

But better than all of this, we shall look into Jesus' face, just like Simeon and Anna did. Only this time it will not be into the face of a baby, but into the face of the One who gave His life for our salvation – the King of Kings and Lord of Lords.

The wait will be worth it.

"For now we see in a mirror dimly, but then face to face. Now I know in part; then I shall know fully, even as I have been fully known."
1 Corinthians 13:12

Ageing: Taking a closer look

For personal or group study

Study questions

1 Read Luke 2:22–38 and acquaint yourself with the main characters in this story.
2 What do you admire about Anna? Is it possible to be too passionate about God?
3 Simeon was well known for hearing God speak (Luke 2:26). He had spiritual ears. How can we hear God speak today? Start your investigation with John 10:27 and Mark 4:24.
4 Meditate on Amos 3:7. Why, and how, does God reveal His plans to His servants? Use other Scriptures to back up your answer.
5 Damage to our reputation can be devastating. Jesus' words in Luke 6:27–28 are difficult to put into practice. Perhaps now is a good time to pray for the courage to obey.
6 "Wait for the LORD; be strong, and let your heart take courage; wait for the LORD!" These words from Psalm 27:14 are a powerful encouragement to choose patience, and build our trust in God. Which Scriptures encourage you to "wait for the LORD"?
7 Simeon and Anna are wonderful examples of how God willingly uses us in our old age. Promises found in Psalm 92:12–15, Isaiah 46:4 and Acts 2:17 endorse that God still has a place for the older generation in His plan today. Allow that truth to sink in.
8 Praise was Simeon and Anna's response on the day they met Jesus. What will be your response when you look into His face one day (Acts 1:11)? If you are not prepared for that meeting, then get ready by taking your Bible and follow the Romans' route to salvation... Romans 3:23, 6:23, 5:8, and 10:9–10, 13.

Notes

1   Emily Owen, *God's Calling Cards*, Authentic Media, 2019, p. 77,

2   Max Lucado, "No Failure is Fatal", https://www.faithgateway.com/no-failure-fatal/, 4 February 2017.

3   United Nations, Universal Declaration of Human Rights, https://www.un.org/en/universal-declaration-human-rights/, 1948.

4   Augustine of Hippo, *The Confessions of Saint Augustine*, Book 1, p. 1.

5   Don Straka, "Do you excuse your own sin?", Desiring God, 8 November 2017, www.desiringgod.org/articles/do-you-excuse-your-own-sin.

6   Joe Carter, "What is Conscience?", Gospel Coalition, 4 March 2014, https://www.thegospelcoalition.org/article/what-is-conscience/.

7   Max Lucado, "God's Patience", www.maxlucado.com/listen/gods-patience-2/, 4 May 2017.

8   John Piper, "What Is Hope?", www.desiringgod.org/messages/what-is-hope, 6 April 1986.

9   Hymn, *The Solid Rock*, Edward Mote, 1834, public domain.

Other Books by Catherine Campbell

Journey with Me

Under the Rainbow

Broken Works Best

Rainbows for Rainy Days

God Knows Your Name

Chasing the dawn

When We Can't, God Can